*The Desert Sentinels*

*Also by Kenneth L. Bjorgum:*
THE BETRAYED

# The
# Desert
# Sentinels

KENNETH L. BJORGUM

DOUBLEDAY & COMPANY, INC.
GARDEN CITY, NEW YORK
1980

All of the characters in this book are fictitious,
and any resemblance to actual persons,
living or dead, is purely coincidental.

Library of Congress Cataloging in Publication Data

Bjorgum, Kenneth.
　　The desert sentinels.

　　I. Title.
PZ4.B6259De　　[PS2552.J56]　　813'.54
ISBN: 0-385-14752-X
Library of Congress Catalog Card Number 79-6640
Copyright © 1980 by Kenneth L. Bjorgum
All Rights Reserved
Printed in the United States of America
*First Edition*

*To Carol and Greg, with thanks
for their patience and dedication*

*The Desert Sentinels*

## Chapter One

The proud, deep-chested roan pranced its measured gait along the deserted street, followed by a packhorse ranging to one side on a length of lead rope. Fetlock-deep dust powdered around each carefully placed hoof, and the horse rolled its jaw under constant bit pressure and arched its neck defiantly against the reins as the smell of fresh water and grain reached its flared nostrils. The confused bawl of penned cattle rolled through the sullen afternoon quiet of Abilene, and the horse cantered sideways in a display of impatience. Firm hands held the horse in check while uncompromising eyes continued to watch the holding pens from beneath the lowered brim of a wide, sweat-stained Stetson.

There was a hardness about the lean rider's handsome face, and the restless anger in his dark eyes was deepened by the brown stubble along his taut jaw, the hair turned near black against sun-bronzed skin. His right hand rested lightly on his thigh with palm cupped toward the butt of a Colt Forty-four dangling from his hip while the stock of a Winchester bobbed gently in the saddle scabbard. Weather-bleached chaps encased long legs and a Bull Durham tag bounced in a dancing jangle from the breast pocket of the vest hung loosely across his muscular chest.

With a nearly imperceptible motion of the reins, the rider turned his horse toward the holding pens and studied the brand on the cow nearest to him. Burned as thin black stripes in tan hide, the letters, LKJ, were easily visible, and a faint smile touched the corners of his mouth and the eyes flickered with a glint of anticipation.

Two young trail men stepped from behind the pen, and with a whoop, waved their advance money in the air while hurrying toward The Longhorn saloon with the stiff-legged strides of men who had spent many days in the saddle. The rider nudged his horse and moved up beside them.

"You boys work for the LKJ ranch down near Waco?" he asked, offering cordiality.

The taller of the two men looked up with indifference and spoke without breaking stride. "We ain't boys, mister. We just done drove a herd of cattle from Texas to this here waterin' hole. Boys don't do that kind of work."

The horse kept pace with their long strides. "No, guess they don't," the rider allowed, with a light smile. "Who's the ramrod?"

"Barkley."

The rider nodded and the smile faded in instant disappointment. "How 'bout a man name Lane? Hank Lane?"

"Never heard of him."

They were nearing the saloon now, and the trail hands hurried quickly onto the boardwalk and the smaller man turned back at the batwing doors and offered an apologetic grin. "Ain't got time for chit-chat, old-timer. We've got a terrible big thirst that's in need of some drownin'."

The rider nodded and smiled inwardly at the thought of being called an "old-timer." Then, while the horses moved forward and sucked greedily at the water trough, disappointment flooded through his brain. Hank Lane was the last one left, and he had been certain of finding him here in Abilene.

He swung to the ground and draped the reins over the crossbar of the hitching rail and stepped onto the boardwalk with a gentle clinking of spurs. The odor of beer and whiskey mingled with tobacco smoke wafting over the batwing doors, and the sound of drunken voices drifted out to him. Memories of another time, long ago, flitted through his mind as he stepped inside.

Elbowing his way through the crowded room, he found a

vacant place at the bar and watched patiently as the bartender furiously poured beer and measured out whiskey. When the thick-bodied man worked his way close enough to be heard, the rider said in a voice just strong enough to be heard, "I'd like a double whiskey, beer back, when you get the time."

"Wait your turn," the harried barkeep returned, filling three mugs in one hand. "I only got two arms"—he risked a sideways glance—"and I . . ." His jaw dropped and his mouth hung open and he stared in silence for several seconds. His mouth moved in a futile attempt at speech while he shoved the mugs across and hurriedly began wiping his hands on the apron around his middle. "Well I'll be go to hell! I can't believe it! Blake! Blake Evans!"

"In the flesh. Howdy, Bill," Blake grinned. "See you're still charming people with your wit and wisdom."

"What are you doin' back here?" the bartender asked, pumping Blake's hand wildly before turning to get his drinks. "Thought you'd be home building that ranch for your ma and pa. How long's it been? Two, maybe three years now?"

Blake nodded as the glasses were pushed before him. "Closer to three, Bill." He stared deeply into the amber liquid and the hardness was in his eyes again. "Wasn't anything to go home for," he said quietly, raising the glass to his lips. "Took me three years to settle up some debts." He drank and his eyes surveyed the room. "Looks like things have changed a bit since I was here last."

The bartender agreed with a hint of sadness in his voice. "They have, Blake. When you and old Hank and Whit and the rest of the boys brought up those first herds back in sixty-three, there was excitement and adventure about it. Nobody'd ever drove a thousand head of cattle that far before. Now, every trail bum in the country's doin' it. Business is booming and the town's gone to hell."

Blake's eyes brightened with the mention of his old trail comrades. "What about the old crew, Bill? Thought I'd catch up with Hank here."

The bartender shook his head. "Haven't seen Hank in a year or better. Just didn't show up one spring and . . . hey! There is one of the old gang still left. Remember Andy?"

"Best damned little drag man that ever sat a horse."

"He'll agree with you on that," the bartender chuckled, pointing out a table in a corner at the rear. "There he is, passed out in all his glory, as usual."

Blake turned and a broad smile split his lips when he found the thin, elderly man sprawled across a chair, head back and snoring softly.

"Give me a bottle, will you, Bill?" Blake asked, dragging some bills from his pocket. "I'd better wake old Andy up before he chokes on the flies."

The bartender shoved the bottle and another glass across but waved the money aside. "This is on me, Blake. Just seeing you again makes me remember the old times, and that's more than worth the price of a bottle. Go talk with Andy and I'll see you later."

Blake crossed the room and stared down at the bandy-legged little drag rider. The lines etched deeply in his leathered face were carved by the hand of time and sealed by blistering sun and stinging wind. He seemed ancient and ageless at the same time, and to Blake's eyes, unchanged. He grinned and popped the cork from the bottle, then aimed a tiny trickle of whiskey into the open mouth.

"What the . . . what . . . who do you . . ." the old rider spluttered, coughing and trying to scramble to his feet. Blake placed a hand on his shoulder and held him fast to the chair.

"If I was a snake, I could've bit you, Andy. How've you been, you old lush?"

Andy coughed once more and wiped the moisture from his eyes with the back of a hand. He looked up through blurred vision and his lips barely moved. "Blake? Is that you, Blake Evans?"

"Yeah, it's me, Andy."

The old man's head moved with disbelieving slowness.

"God bless these old eyes, boy. Never thought I'd see you again."

Blake pulled up a chair and eased down. "I didn't think you would either, Andy. I didn't plan on coming back."

Andy studied the somber look on Blake's face and found an answer that precluded questions. "Things didn't work out at home, huh?" he said simply, asking nothing.

"No. No, they sure didn't. Here, you old crowbait, sit up and have a drink and tell me about the old crew.'

Blake filled the glasses while Andy struggled to a sitting position and adjusted his hat. "Not much to tell, Blake. Some's dead, others is drifted with a tailing wind."

Blake's eyes narrowed with the word "dead" and he lowered his voice to flat tones and prepared his mind for the worst. "You said dead, Andy. Who's dead?"

"Brandy. Horse fall. Barney. Blood poisinin'. Church was killed . . . you didn't know old Church, did you, Blake?"

Blake shook his head and relief flooded through his brain. He wanted to ask about one man, but he would have to come last. "How about Whitlow?"

"Meaner'n ever, if that's possible. He gave up trailin' cows a couple-a seasons ago. Mr. Samuelson's gettin' kinda old and asked Whit to run the LKJ."

"How about Rodrigo and Biggie Munn?" Blake asked, while a vivid image of the two wranglers flashed through his mind. Gauchos they had called themselves. Strange, fierce men from some distant country called Argentina. Rodrigo was all he was known by and he was easily the most intelligent and deadly man Blake had ever known. Driven from his homeland by revolution, with his entire family dead at the hands of federal troops, he was a man of the land with a strange inner strength and self-confidence. He spoke only when words were necessary, and when they weren't, he remained silent as though yearning for the wild, open country. Cat-quick with either revolver or knife, as well as with the ever-present bola—three hard leather balls attached to leather thongs—he swiftly killed those who were "In death's debt." The words rang in Blake's ears as though Rodrigo were speaking to him again.

And Biggie Munn. A gigantic nomad whom Rodrigo referred to as a gypsy. Towering above tall men with the muscles across his chest and shoulders corded like the rolling sinews on a bull's neck, he was equally as deadly as Rodrigo even though his pale blue eyes danced with laughing humor. But it was the sucking noise that Blake remembered most. The sound made by a big, hearty man laughing with half his tongue cut out and the red stump wagging behind gold-inlaid teeth. A tongue cut out by those same government troops who had killed Rodrigo's family.

"Are they gone too?"

"Yeah. Went to Mexico. Rodrigo said he had a friend there, a fella name Juárez, who was fighting a revolution or some idiotic thing. They went to help him out. Best damned help that guy is ever gonna get," Andy concluded, draining his glass and brushing a sleeve across his lips as he spoke again. "Remember that night just after we crossed the Yellow River and Swede went down? When them renegades jumped us? If it hadn't been for Rod and Munn, we'd both be starin' straight up at dirt right now."

Blake nodded, remembering the night. The huge, filthy, red-haired soldier named Garth, holding a cup of fresh cow's blood in his hands. Drinking it and pawing the goo from his beard with lusty relish. Then refilling the cup and handing it to Blake. "Drink up, boy," he had said, "or yer friend here ain't gonna be wearin' a head no more." Even now, Blake's stomach twisted into tight knots when he mentally tasted the acrid, warm liquid again. And, later that night, he carefully squeezed the trigger on the Colt in his trembling hands and sent a bullet to smash the life from the man named Garth.

A shudder ran up Blake's spine and he quickly changed the subject. "What about old Shoo? He still cookin' for the LKJ?"

Andy laughed. "Yeah, if you want to call it that. Stays at the main ranch now, too old for the trail, I guess." He sobered and looked away. "So am I, Blake. This is my last round. It just ain't the same no more."

"Gotta be an end to everything sometime, Andy. What've you got in mind to do?"

The old trail hand snorted and filled the glass again. "You ain't gonna believe this, 'cause I still don't, but Whit wants me to help that miserable jackass known as the Honorable Carl Francis Schooster in the cookhouse." He drank and his face twisted as if the whiskey had gone sour. "Peelin' spuds and stuff like that."

Blake chuckled as he thought of the two old adversaries in the same kitchen. "You gonna do it?"

"Suppose so," Andy shrugged. "Leastwise, till I learn to cook well enough to run Shoo off."

Blake chuckled again, but his mind was on the last man now. He toyed with his glass pensively before speaking. "What about Hank, Andy," he asked softly. "Bill told me he hasn't shown up in quite a while."

Andy studied the young man across from him, aged beyond his years. "You and Hank was pretty close, weren't you, Blake?"

Blake nodded, lips tight. "Yeah. Real close. Almost like brothers, you might say. He's the closest thing I've got to family now."

"Sorry to hear that, Blake. Not about Hank, but about your family."

Blake nodded again and waited in silence.

"Last time I saw old Hank was just before this drive started three months or so back. He was just passin' through and stopped by the ranch for some hot grub and a bath. Said he'd been to New Orleans and hit it big in a poker game. Won hisself a silver mine named The Lucky Lady or some damned thing. Was headed out west to strike it rich."

Blake leaned forward with a start and whiskey spilled over the sides of his glass. "Where out west?"

"Arizona Territory. Said the mine was about three days' ride from an army post called Fort Hastings. Not too far from

Mexico, I guess. He had the deed, map and all. He was happy as a speckled pup in a chicken coop. Said he was just gonna take his time gettin' there 'cause there wasn't no need for a rich man's gettin' in a hurry." Andy leaned back and chuckled. "Old Hank's the damnedest character I ever met. Don't care whether school takes up or not."

Blake downed his drink in a single gulp and pushed away from the table. "Which direction is this Arizona Territory from here, Andy?"

"Hey, where the hell ya goin'? Ain't ya even gonna help me finish off this bottle afore you take off?"

"Can't do it, Andy. I've gotta find Hank. And since I'm not a rich man like him, I haven't got time to waste," Blake said with a grin. "Now, which direction?"

"Southwest. Fifteen, maybe twenty days' ride."

"Thanks, Andy. What say we ride part way together?"

Andy smiled weakly, but his gaze drifted to the window. "I'd like to ride with ya, Blake, but I think I'll hold off a few more days. Like I done said, this is my last time around the woodshed. I've had a saddle horn in front of me since before I could walk proper, and it's kinda hard ta think it's over. When I gets myself back to Texas from this one, I won't be a man no more. I'd kinda like to put that off a spell. Long as I can, anyway."

Blake smiled warmly and offered his hand which Andy eagerly accepted. "I can understand that, Andy. Mighty good to see you again. And, take care of yourself, okay?"

The old man's eyes misted and he blinked angrily at the tears. "Get on with ya. I don't need no kids worryin' over me."

Blake turned and walked quickly to the door, but stopped when he heard the graveled voice coming from the table behind him.

"Stop by the ranch sometime, Blake. I'll cook you up the flattest batch of biscuits you ever saw."

"I'll do that, Andy," Blake said with a wave before pushing through the batwing doors.

## Chapter Two

Colonel Nevis Bibby held the fork poised over the thick, porcelain plate. He watched the beads of grease congeal around the last morsel of salt pork and his ample stomach rumbled a warning. Laying the fork down, and after a cursory touching of napkin to lips, Bibby allowed his fingers to explore the expanding girth above his waistline, as they did after each meal. With a heavy sigh, he leaned back in the hard wooden chair and looked around the headquarters building of Fort Hastings. God, he thought, how I hate this place! A man serves garrison duty throughout the entire war, never sees combat, hates service in the field and tries to be a gentleman throughout. And where does it get him? A commanding assignment to the most Godforsaken hell hole on earth.

He thought about Fort Hastings. A small outpost with two hundred troops and situated, in Bibby's opinion, too damned close to Mexico. What they had come to call The Outlaw Trail was but a day's ride to the east, hostile Indian bands ranged to the north, and horse thieves and smugglers filtered across the land like ghosts through a graveyard. And we, he reminded himself with a comforting smirk, are supposed to maintain law and order and establish the territory as a peaceful, patriotic adjunct to the sovereigns of the United States of America. Not to mention maintaining safe and secure transportation lanes for the numerous silver mines in the area to move their precious metal from Arizona to California and thence by schooner around the cape to Boston.

Impossible! Bibby reminded himself with a firm rap of his knuckles on the table top. Impossible, ridiculous and out of the question! And certainly not the job for a senior officer whose primary field of experience is in quartermaster services. Hell, I haven't had my dress uniform on since I got here, and I doubt, should the occasion arise, which it won't, that the damned thing would fit anyway, what with the deplorable food and absence of polo fields.

Bibby reached for a cigar, struck a match and watched the flame near the blunt tip, but his mind was on Captain Mathew Stearns, his replacement and now three days overdue. He knew little about Stearns and cared less, except that the captain was his ticket out of Fort Hastings. Nothing else mattered, as long as the man could sit a horse, give commands and salute after he had received the flag in the change-of-command ceremonies. Beyond that, he's on his own, Bibby concluded firmly, and so is the Arizona Territory with its weird accumulation of crawling, biting, stinging, poisonous creatures with people to match.

He picked up the telegram and read it for the hundredth time. Its content informed Colonel Nevis Bibby that a Captain Mathew Stearns was being sent as his replacement. He would be accompanied by a detachment of twenty and escorting a wagon that contained items of extreme military and political significance to the United States Government. The detachment would be permanently assigned to Fort Hastings. They would be bringing their service records, extra uniforms and weapons. With the exception of officers and non-coms, the troops were being sent to the outpost as a disciplinary action in lieu of court-martial.

Bibby tossed the telegram to one side and rubbed an infant ash from his cigar. "Good luck, Captain Stearns," he said softly in the stilled room. "You are definitely going to need it. Especially if anyone finds out what's in that wagon you're escorting." Rising, Bibby crossed the room on heavy-legged strides and surveyed a huge wall map while one hand went behind his back to rest knuckles against spine in a proper military stance.

That's something our government should never have done,

as if I didn't have enough problems already, he thought as his eyes swept over the Mexican border. Stearns is bringing out three hundred of our finest Spencer repeating rifles, three hundred, for Christ's sake, to give to some revolutionary rabble headed toward the fort at this very moment. What was his name again? Juárez? Yes, that's it, Benito Pablo Juárez. Why? Because the big thinkers in Washington think it would be in the best interest of the nation to see Maximilian overthrown. "A lot they know," Bibby muttered, shrugging his sloping shoulders irritatedly. What the hell's the big deal? They're both Mexicans, and that says all that needs to be said. The only difference is, two snakes in your pocket are worse than one.

Weary of it all, Bibby turned and his eye fell upon the whiskey bottle beside his nightstand. He hesitated, warning himself. His thick fingers passed over dry lips and he moved toward the bottle. Sure it's a little early, he allowed, but who the hell is going to know? Out here, time is meaningless, as is everything else. One short drink is all I need, and I'm damned well going to have it.

He tried to control the trembling in his hands as the cork came free. Glass rattled against glass and a few drops of amber liquid splashed on the floor. Finally, the glass was a quarter full and Bibby gulped the drink just as a loud pounding came upon the door. Quickly replacing the cork, Bibby puffed furiously on his cigar for several seconds while taking a seat at the desk. He scrounged for some papers to look over, then glanced toward the door.

"Who is it?"

"Corporal Darby, sir!" The soldier's voice was muffled by heavy wood. "There's somethin' out here that you might better come take a look at, sir!"

An apprehensive expression crossed Bibby's face. "Come in, Corporal, damnit! We can't talk through the door!"

Darby burst into the room and threw a hasty salute. "Mornin', Colonel. Sorry to bother you but . . ."

"But what? Get to the point, young man!"

"Detachment's comin', sir. Or, what's left of it."

A deeper apprehension was there now, and it twisted Bibby's pale face into a look of dread as he struggled ponderously to his feet. But his mind, in contrast with his body, seized upon its greatest fear: something had happened to Captain Stearns. Damn the luck!

Brushing the corporal aside, Bibby wallowed across the parade ground like an overfed bear. And by the time he had climbed the stairs to the top of the parapet, his sides were heaving in co-ordination with gasped gulps of air. The corporal bounded up the steps behind him and pointed to the northeast. Bibby's eyes followed the extended finger and his heart sank.

Seven riders were approaching at a steady lope. The blue and yellow colors of the United States Cavalry were visible on six of the men while the seventh, dressed in civilian clothes, sat straight and tall in the saddle. His hands were tied behind his back and his horse ranged behind the others on a long lead rope.

"Thought there were supposed to be twenty replacements and a supply wagon, sir," Darby said, cautiously.

"You're damned right there were, Corporal!" Bibby snapped, his eyes searching for the captain's insignia on the lead rider and not finding it. "Get down there and open the main gates. If Stearns isn't leading that command, then let's hope to hell one of them is an officer at least. Get going, man!"

Darby scrambled down the steps and Bibby followed carefully with one hand tracing the guard rail. The gates swung wide and what remained of the detachment galloped into the compound on sweat-streaked horses before pulling up hard. The lead rider swung down and sunlight glinted off his now-visible twin captain's bars. Bibby sighed heavily and leaned momentarily against the wall for support. Then he approached the captain while displaying his most severe military countenance.

The captain ordered his troops to dismount and Bibby surveyed them as they formed a ragged line. Their uniforms were torn and splotched with blood. Unshaven faces surrounded vacant eyes, and Bibby knew he was looking at the hardest men ever to disgrace an army uniform. With the exception of the captain. He was a young man of medium build, but powerfully constructed. A blond moustache graced his upper lip, and he held himself ramrod straight while his gloved hand snapped against the brim of his hat in a crisp salute. The others complied with desultory ineptness while the seventh man remained tied to his saddle and looking down with cold, contemptuous eyes. Bibby glanced at the civilian before waving the salute away and was startled by the look of haughty superiority on the captive's face. Then Bibby concentrated on the captain.

"Captain Stearns?"

"Yes, sir! Captain Mathew Stearns." The young officer's eyes wavered neither right nor left as he stared straight ahead. "Sorry we're late, sir."

"That you are, Captain. Please, be at ease," Bibby said, watching Stearns' body automatically flow into the at-ease position which, to the colonel, didn't seem to be at ease at all. "What has happened to your detachment and, for the love of God, where is the wagon you were sent to protect?"

"We were ambushed, sir. Sixteen troopers killed, the wagon stolen."

"Stolen! Do you have any idea what was in . . ." Bibby caught himself. "Who ambushed you, and who is that civilian?"

"I don't know who ambushed us, Colonel. But I do know that he was the leader. He denies it. Says he's a miner." The captain's hat tilted toward the man in the saddle. "Does he look like a miner to you, sir?"

Bibby studied the young man again. Hard features, hating eyes. Slim, tall and muscular. Seated on a magnificent horse with roping saddle. An empty rifle scabbard lay beneath his left leg and his clothes were dust free where a gun belt had been removed. No, Bibby concluded automatically, he does not look like a miner. He stepped toward the rider, but the captain stopped him.

"It's no use, Colonel. I've questioned him at length, but he won't change his story. Sixteen of my men were killed in the initial assault. He had at least thirty men with him, renegades, bandits and the like. In the interest of my men, I surrendered. They drove off our horses and took our weapons before leaving with the wagon. It took us the better part of the day to catch the horses again, but when we did, we established pursuit immediately. Their trail was easy to follow until we got to the river, then it vanished. But one horse had left the others just before the river so we trailed it."

The captain turned to glare at the silent rider. "Apparently he thought he was safe, because when we caught up with him he was asleep in an abandoned mine. After we overpowered him and brought him into the light, I recognized him immediately, as did the others. He was the leader of the renegades. And this," the captain turned and jerked an army Spencer from his saddle, "was in his possession."

Bibby's fleshy eyes narrowed as he looked at the rifle. Then he turned and stepped toward the rider. "Where have your men gone with the wagon?"

The rider's lips curled into a sneer and he spat contemptuously. "Your soldier boy there is a liar. I don't know what he's trying to pull off, but he's got the wrong man. I wasn't near his detachment. I ride alone, and I've never seen him nor any of this other collection of scum before in my life."

The captain spun toward the rider and his eyes blazed. "If you weren't under military arrest, I'd kill you on the spot for calling me a liar!"

"A spade is a spade," the rider said, his tone cold and deadly.

Bibby's jowls trembled and he stepped back slightly. "Now hold on there," he managed, his voice less than commanding. "Name calling from either side will do no good. Captain Stearns, I am quite in agreement with you. If that man is a miner, I'm John the Apostle. He will be tried in a court of law and hanged if the judgment goes against him, as I'm sure it will." The colonel looked at the steely-eyed man and tried to soften his voice. "What's your name, son?"

The rider pursed his lips and spat. Bibby stumbled backward and the spittle splashed across one of his highly polished boots. The rider smiled and raised his shoulder to touch his shirt to the corner of his mouth. Then he glared down and his tone was searingly emphatic.

"I own The Lucky Lady silver mine, and there ain't no fatherless bastard like you who's gonna see me hang for something I didn't do." He hesitated and his eyes burned twin holes on Bibby's face. "And in answer to your question, my name's Hank Lane."

## Chapter Three

They rode north and their horses clattered across the rocky bottom of the shallow river known as the Rio Grande. In a column of twos, twelve riders, followed by two heavily laden packhorses, moved steadily into the flat desert land of the Arizona Territory. They rode silently, each with determination etched on their sun-bronzed faces. Dark moustaches drooped from the lips of all but one, sombreros bobbed with the horses' strides and well-oiled weapons rested in saddle scabbards and on narrow hips. They were lean, hard men and they appeared to be tireless as they rode. But, even in the similarity, there was a difference in the two lead riders.

The man on the left, riding a powerful black stallion, had a deadliness about him that the other could not match. His eyes searched the desert before them in restless sweeps and the firmness of his lips spoke of hard years and pain. The long knife on his left hip countered the weight of the revolver on his right, and from his saddle horn dangled three round objects made of the hardest leather and attached to long thongs. And, he was dwarfed by his companion.

Riding a huge gray horse, he was in complete contrast with those who followed. His eyes were sky-blue and contained a hint of humor. His complexion was fair but deeply tanned, and he was massive in size. The muscles across his shoulders and arms were corded knots of latent power and his thick arms might have been thighs on another man. His shirt was open across a massive chest and bulging biceps pressed against strained cotton. A loop of gold dangled from his left ear and his head was shaven beneath the spreading sombrero.

A rider behind spoke rapidly in Spanish, condemning the fact that they were riding away from tequila instead of toward it. Biggie Munn threw his head back and laughed. His gold-inlaid teeth glittered in the sunlight and a sucking gurgle was muffled by the hammering of hooves on packed earth.

Rodrigo looked across and might have smiled. "That is true, Cassildo," he said loudly enough for all to hear. "But whiskey will not make you quite so crazy. In two days we will have our rifles and return to the land of tequila and beautiful women." His face sobered and he looked to the north again. "And to the land of revolution," he said quietly, before falling silent.

## Chapter Four

The awakening desert spread before him as though a rainbow had splashed upon the ground. Blake Evans reined in his horse to stare in silent awe at the magnificent beauty of the desert at daybreak. An endless wasteland of fantastically brilliant colors. Comprised of buttes, mesas, pinnacles and valleys, it came alive with an incredible array of hues ranging from blues to reds to yellows and greens and offset by shadows of the deepest black. What had that missionary called it when he had asked for directions? El Desierto Pintado? Yes, that was it. The painted desert.

Blake watched the sun surge above the horizon and listened to the dying calls and screeches of desert creatures ceasing their persistent quest of prey to wait out the blazing day for yet another night's hunt. And he pressed the horse forward to continue his hunt until the merciless sun drove him to sanctuary to await the welcome cool of evening. He had been twenty days in the saddle and the missionary had told him he was but two days' ride from Fort Hastings and the small community of Twin Buttes. There, he was sure, he would find out the location of The Lucky Lady silver mine.

The horse picked a winding course through the abandoned land, and even though Blake was impatient to find Hank, he allowed the fine animal to choose its own pace. While not entirely familiar with the desert and its secrets, he could plainly see that a man afoot would quickly be consumed by the all-encompassing silence.

The sun hung hot and low on the horizon as Blake's horses plodded down what passed for the main street of Twin

Buttes. He allowed the animals to stop at the nearest watering trough, and while they drank he bathed his face and hands in the tepid water. Finally, he straightened and wiped his face on the bandanna around his neck while his eyes swept over the town. A blacksmith's shop, a general store, two saloons and a church were rooted precariously on the desert floor. The eyes stopped on another man-made object, a contraption he had never seen before. Obviously newly constructed with green planking, it was a stilted platform with several steps leading from the ground upward. Two side beams supported a center beam ten feet above the platform and a rope hung from that top beam with a loop open just below a series of tight knots. Blake stared at the ominous creation in mild horror and realized he was looking at a hanging gallows. A shiver tickled up his spine and he took up the reins again and led his horses toward the saloon. As he went down the street he passed through the lengthening shadow of the gallows and an eerie, almost panicked sensation passed through his mind.

He stepped into the saloon and the noise and laughter, the sounds of people, alive and uncaring, made him glad to be off the naked street.

"What'll it be?" the bartender asked when Blake leaned against the rail.

"Beer and a whiskey."

"Comin' up."

Blake glanced around the room and saw mostly miners, raw-boned and strangely pale, lined up at the bar and seated at tables. Five soldiers were crowded around a table in the corner, and their loud laughter and vulgar language served as indication of the advanced stage of their drunkenness. A beer mug thumped down and Blake turned back to drain the mug with long, thirsty swallows before tipping the whiskey. The bartender watched silently as Blake pushed the glasses across again and pulled a bill from his pocket.

"I've been dreaming about that beer for more than a week now," Blake offered. "Better do the same thing again, huh?"

"Your stomach," the bartender countered, watching Blake

as he poured. "Appears you've been in the saddle quite a while."

"Yeah, that's a fact."

"Where you from? Don't think I've seen you in here before."

"You haven't. Just rode in. I'm not really from anyplace, but Abilene, Kansas, will do."

The barkeep shoved the drinks across and made change. "Abilene, huh? There's a pretty piece of distance between here and there. Come down to strike it rich in the mines?"

Blake grinned as the mug moved toward his lips again. "You might say that. Friend of mine's got a mine somewhere near here. Ever here of The Lucky Lady?"

Furrowing his brow, the bartender tried to think. "No, can't say that I have, but there's so damned many holes around here that these guys call mines that I can't remember 'em all. Might ask one of the moles here at the bar."

"Yeah, I'll do that. Thanks."

The bartender began toweling the plank off and asked amicably, "You gonna stay for the hangin', aren't you?"

Blake subdued a shudder. "No, no, don't think I will."

"Better do it. Folks is comin' from all around just to see the show. Pretty big doin's for Twin Buttes."

Blake remained silent and wondered why anyone would want to see another man hang. The bartender mistook his silence as one of consideration.

"Gonna be a big day, tomorrow is. Everybody's bringin' picnic lunches, we're gonna have foot races for the kids and a quarter-mile horse race for the grown-ups." He pointed toward the soldiers. "See that young fella over there?" Blake looked and nodded. "He's a captain, and after the hangin' tomorrow he'll be in command out at the fort. He's challenged one and all to a race, and the others there at the table are takin' all bets. You look like a cowboy. If you've got a good horse you just might be able to pick up a few bucks."

Blake shook his head, but his eyes remained on the soldiers. He could see the captain's face clearly but the others had their backs toward him and he couldn't see their faces. One was a very large man with a ruthless laugh and, somehow, there was a strange familiarity about him. Then he looked away and sipped his whiskey.

"Nope, not much for racing," Blake said. "Not the right thing to do to a good horse. Just like makin' a party out of watchin' a man hang isn't my idea of a party."

"Captain Stearns wouldn't agree with you on that last remark. About two weeks ago a band of outlaws jumped his detachment comin' out from Saint Jo. Killed sixteen of his troopers. Stearns caught the leader, they gave him a legal trial, and tomorrow he's gonna see his last sunrise."

Blake shrugged. "Seems that would be a military affair. Why are they making a circus out of it?"

The bartender smiled and casually picked a scab on his forearm. "Captain Stearns' idea, the way I hear it. Since he's gonna be in charge out at the fort from now on, he figures everybody should see what happens to the man who kills a trooper. And I agree. The army's about the only decent law we got around here, with the exception of Ned Hanson, our sheriff."

Blake was tiring of the conversation. "Maybe you're right, but I don't think a man's being hung is any good reason for a picnic. Nice talkin' to ya," Blake said, turning away.

"Sure, anytime. If you're still around tomorrow, come out and see the fun. Don't think Lane would mind another set of eyes watchin' him dance at the end of a rope."

Blake froze in his tracks. Stunned, his mind whirled and he repeated the name he thought he had heard. His face remained calm but his mind was ablaze. Lane? Did he say Lane? He turned back toward the bartender. "What was that name again?"

"Lane. Hank Lane. Leastwise that's what he told the judge. Christ only knows what his real name is. At any rate, he's sittin' in a jail cell at the edge of town hoping the sun won't come up in the morning. Why? You heard of him?"

Blake fought for control. "No, no I haven't. Just curious, that's all. Night."

He stumbled on the first step, caught himself and looked around to see if anyone had noticed. They hadn't and he led his horses away with frantic desperation raging in his mind. Hank? They're gonna hang Hank? God, no! Not Hank! A cold-blooded killer? They've got the wrong man, and I've gotta get him out of this. But how? How the hell do you break someone out of jail? I don't know, but by God I'll find out how. He glanced at the small building on the far end of town and a final thought passed through his brain: or maybe wind up beside him tomorrow morning?

After tying his horses to the last hitching rail, Blake moved cautiously but not suspiciously toward the jail. With the sun now down, he could see lamplight spilling from the front window and he walked by the open door almost on tiptoes. He glanced in and saw the balding man seated behind his desk and going over some paperwork. "Damn," he muttered, passing through the yellow light and into the darkness beyond. He considered drawing his Colt and forcing the sheriff to open the door but quickly discarded the idea. That would have to be a last resort.

He circled the building, and pressing his back to the rough adobe bricks, crept toward a barred window just above his head in the center of the wall. As he approached he heard the blurred, slurred words of a song being softly sung by someone obviously intoxicated.

"I met a gal . . . a gal her name was . . . Sal . . . down by the moonlight river. She . . ."

Blake smiled in the darkness. Singing that bad could only come from one man.

"Pssssssst! Hank!" he said almost under his breath with a nervous glance in either direction.

Nothing, but the singing stopped.

"Hank! It's me . . ."

"Get the hell out of here, damn you!"

"Shhhhh. It's me . . ."

"I said get, damnit! I got no prayers to pray and nobody to waste 'em on! Get the hell away from here or I'll have the good sheriff . . ."

"What the hell's going on back there?"

"Somebody's tryin' to break into my little room here, sheriff. Get off your ass and do your job. Arrest the sonofabitch!"

Blake sprinted away, catching the shadows and working his way back to town. Same old Hank: drunk and uncooperative, just like always. How the hell . . . then a thought struck him. Dynamite. Sure, that's it! Dynamite! This was a mining town, and they used the stuff all the time. Never used it before, but it didn't look all that difficult. Fuse, stick and match. But where to get it and how much to use? Just then he saw the merchant locking up the general store for the night and raced across the street.

"Excuse me, sir," he said as the merchant turned away from the door, "but you've got to help me. I need some things from your store real bad."

The storekeeper adjusted his glasses and hiked his receipt books beneath his arm. "Sorry, young man. The store is closed. Come back at eight o'clock in the morning. No, make that nine. I'll be at the hanging at eight."

Blake grabbed the elderly man's arm. "You've got to help me. My partner's trapped. A shaft collapsed. I've gotta get him out or he'll die. I need some dynamite."

The merchant eyed him suspiciously. "Why don't you get some of the other miners to help you? Surely they must know what to do."

Blake shook his head vigorously. "No, I can't do that. My partner's a real stubborn sort. We've struck a dandy vein, and he'd rather die than have anybody find out where we're working. You've got to help me."

The storekeeper hesitated, jerked his watch fob and checked the time, then heaved a heavy sigh. "How much do you need?"

"Six sticks should do it."

"Cash?"

"Cash. Plus a little extra for your time."

The merchant nodded and Blake followed him inside. In the space of ten minutes he was back on the street with six sticks of dynamite and a length of fuse. Knowing the clerk would be watching, he crossed to his horses and pretended to be stuffing the dynamite into his pack saddle. The storekeeper maintained his vigil for several seconds before hurrying down the street.

Moving at a run now, Blake circled the buildings and went to the far end of town. He measured off three lengths of fuse and guessed. A foot a minute? He made one three feet long, another two feet long and the last a foot. Working with great haste, he planted one behind a hillock, another near the road and the longest fuse some distance away. He was sweating now and his hands were slick as he pressed the powdered wire into soft dynamite. When all three were in place, he took the remaining length of fuse and wrapped it around the sticks left over to make a bundle. He stabbed a short fuse into one of the sticks and sneaked back toward town.

The only horses at the hitching rail were those belonging to the soldiers, so Blake selected the strongest and finest of the five. He led the horse carefully toward the rear of the jail and tied it securely to a cottonwood tree. Then, mounting his own horse, he rode back through town with the pack animal on lead. His shirt was soaked with sweat, and when he stepped down beside the charge farthest away, the matches in his pocket were damp and would not strike. He dug in the pack and found his reserves wrapped in dry canvas. His hands trembled as he touched flame to fuse. There was a spark, a sputter, then the hiss and smell of burning powder. Blake swung into the saddle and spurred toward the next charge which he lit, as well as the third. He felt exhausted for some reason as his foot hit the stirrup again and he swung the horse wide of town at a full gallop.

Slowing to a cautious gait as he neared the jail, he tied his horses beside the cavalry mount and crept back to the wall with the packet of dynamite. And he waited. He counted off a minute and heard nothing but Hank's contented snoring. Come on, goddamnit! It can't be that difficult to blow up a stick of dynamite! He listened and heard nothing. He rubbed his forehead beneath his hat band and leaned against the wall. Don't tell me I'm going to have to go back and . . .

BLLLLLOOOOOOOMMMMMMM!

The concussion of the first stick reverberated through the empty street and there was total silence for several seconds. Wild shouts and yells came from the saloon and he heard the jail office door swing open and bang against the wall. Blake waited. A second explosion ripped the night sky and he heard the sheriff say, "What in the name of . . . ?" before running down the street in the direction of the explosions with the ring of cell keys jangling in his hand. Men poured from the saloon to join the sheriff in his now cautious march down the street. The third blast went off in a roaring flash of light and Blake saw the townsmen dive for cover. He chuckled as he touched a match to the short fuse and laid the packet beside the corner of the building before running back to calm the horses. The three sticks exploded with a deafening roar and the corner of the jail house disappeared in a cloud of dust. Blake ran back and peered through the gloom. Hank's cot was turned on its side and he was crawling along the floor on his hands and knees.

"The rope broke," he muttered, mindless of the dust and debris. "I'll be go to hell, the damned rope broke."

Blake leaped over the rubble and ducked beneath a wooden beam hanging precariously from the ceiling. "Hank! Come on! We've gotta get out of here quick."

Hank blinked and wiped the dust from his eyes. "Who? What?"

"Come on, damnit," Blake hissed. "It's me, Blake."

Hank straightened and stared across the cell as though suddenly frozen. Then he sprang across the room and clapped his hands on Blake's shoulders. "Well now if you aren't a sight for sore eyes, Blakey boy! What are you doin' here?"

"I'm gonna ask that same question of you when I get some

time to ask it. And, I hope your answer is better than mine. Come on, let's go."

They clambered over the fallen adobe and ran in a hunched-over position toward the cottonwood. Men were running toward the jail now and they could hear the angry shouts and exclamations. Blake leaped into his saddle and turned the horse away from the tree while Hank struggled to get his boot into the high, metal stirrup on the military saddle. A shot rang out, followed by several others and Hank vaulted onto the saddle and whipped the horse into an instant gallop while continuing to stab at the stirrups with his boots.

They rode hard deep into the night with Hank in front and Blake following, leading the packhorse. A brisk wind came up and they could see the dust thrown up by their horses' hooves drifting at a sharp, slanting angle. In an hour, no more, they knew their tracks would be obliterated. Hank worked toward the northeast, seeking out flat mesas and plateaus where the rocks and shale were exposed through centuries of incessant wind. The sound of steel-shod hooves on rocks was welcome to their ears while riding a carefully paced escape, sparing the horses while continually moving upward then down again to press the animals harder on the flat valleys.

Hank guided them by direction of the seasoned traveler's most awesome chart; the magnificent galaxies above, naked to the eye of man in the clear, dry air of the vast wastelands. Midnight passed and yet they rode into early morning. The brilliant moon was taking its bedtime plunge toward the horizon when Hank finally pulled up and stepped down before the dark, yawning mouth of a cave. Blake followed suit and they stood, five yards apart. It was the first time they had seen each other in nearly four years.

Hank looked across with his slow, warming smile. "Howdy, Blake. Looks like I owe you one."

Blake dusted his pants legs self-consciously with his hat. "Yeah, Hank. I'd say you do. A big one."

They looked at each other silently and the wind stilled as

the long fingers of pink inched across the desert floor below them. Then they rushed at each other. With each gripping the other's biceps, they did a wild, circling jig until Blake's boot caught on an exposed rock and they fell in a laughing, ecstatic heap. Hank rolled onto one side and struggled to an elbow.

"By God, Blake, you ugly old sonofabitch! I'm so happy to see you I could damned near kiss you."

Blake grinned and the whiteness of his teeth sparkled in the rising sun. "If you do, I'll hang you myself."

"Don't mention that word, boy. Makes my neck hurt." Hank's eyes went to the cavalry mount standing hipshot and exhausted nearby. "And the next time you steal me a horse, how 'bout taking one that's wearing a man's saddle?"

Blake laughed. "That isn't stolen, just borrowed. Besides, the only other choice I had was a miner's donkey. Now that I think about it, I should've took one. Be a real funny sight seeing you ride all this way holdin' your feet off the ground."

"Thanks but no thanks," Hank said, but his eyes were still on the army mount. "Well I'll be damned. You know whose horse that is?"

"Brand says US, so I take it the government is holdin' paper on it."

"That's right enough, but more importantly, it belongs to that bastard who tried to set me up. Captain Mathew Stearns."

Blake remembered the young officer he had seen in the saloon. "Looks like there won't be any race this mornin'."

"What?"

"They were going to have a horse race, with picnic and all to celebrate your departure. The captain was takin' all bets, and I imagine that's the horse he would have rode."

"It's a shame for the guest of honor to run out on his own party, ain't it?" Hank said with a grin.

"What's the deal on all this, Hank? You are innocent, aren't you?"

"Damned right I am! Beyond that, I don't know what the deal is. I was sound asleep, right here in this cave, and dreamin' I was in a helluva lot better place when they jumped me. Stearns said they picked up my trail, which might have been true, but the rest of it sure as Christ isn't."

"What's the rest of it?"

"Stearns positively identified me as the leader of that outlaw gang that ambushed his detachment. You know as well as I do that I wouldn't have a hand in anything like that."

"If I didn't, I wouldn't have blown the hell out of the side of that jail."

"Blow the hell out of it? Man, you destroyed it. Threw me clear across the cell. Next time, let's use half a stick less."

"Listen to this guy," Blake said mockingly, "next time let's use half a stick less. There ain't gonna be no next time, and besides, I never used the damned stuff before. Figured we'd be better off if I used a stick too much than a stick not enough."

Hank laughed easily. "You're right. At least we know how much is a stick too much. I sailed off that cot like I was goin' straight up to heaven. Thought sure they'd hung me and the rope broke. To tell you the truth, I was kind of tickled about it."

"Yeah, and kind of drunk."

"How'd you know that?"

"I was outside your cell. You told the sheriff to arrest me."

"Was that you?"

"Yeah, it was me. How'd you get a bottle of booze in a situation like that?"

"They've got a funny little game they play the night before they hang you. It's called the 'last supper.' Give you anything you want, which of course is whatever they have. Steak and potatoes. Didn't figure I could eat much knowin' what came after that last forkful. I told the sheriff I'd trade my last heartburn for a last hangover. He's a decent enough guy for the business he's in, so he slipped me a quart."

Rich, yellow sunlight now flooded the hillside and Blake looked to the southeast and the desert was deathly calm.

"Think they'll follow us here?" he asked, turning toward Hank again.

"Don't think they can. Pretty good wind last night and we stayed mostly to the rocky ridges. And, I don't think they think I'd be dumb enough to come back here."

"Why did we come back here, if I may be so dumb as to ask?"

A grin flashed across Hank's face. "So we could out-dumb them. Besides, my miner's tools are hidden in the back of the cave. And a spare Colt, which I'm kinda anxious to get next to."

"Your miner's tools? What the hell are you gonna need them for?"

"To work The Lucky Lady, what else?"

"Oh no we're not, Hank! We're clearing out of here just as soon as the horses are rested. I looked at that gallows pretty close, and I know there's room enough for two. Horse stealin' makes me a candidate."

Hank edged forward and there was excitement in his eyes. "We gotta at least take a look at the old girl, Blake! I won the deed from a gambler in . . ."

"I know. Andy told me about it in Abilene."

"So, that's how you found me. Pays to mooch a meal now and then. Anyway, old Larse, the gambler, didn't have anymore money and the stakes were up pretty high. I could see it was killin' him, but he drug the deed to The Lucky Lady out of his pocket. Said it was a working mine over the sweetest vein in all the whole Southwest. A regular glory hole, that's what he called it. I won the hand, and here we are. The old girl's just about ten miles from here and I just gotta see her. Never laid eyes on her yet. You can understand that, can't you, Blake?"

"No. But I guess it wouldn't hurt to take a peek on our way out." He saw the familiar grin on Hank's face and his words became emphatic. "Now just a little look, damn you! Agreed?"

"Agreed. Come on into the cave. I've got some supplies

back there and we'll brew up some coffee and a can of beans. Then, we'll go pick up a couple-a pocketfuls of silver."

Famished, they ate in silence. Blake could feel Hank's eyes upon him and an uneasy tension filled his mind. He knew what was coming and dreaded it.

Hank laid his plate down, rolled a cigarette, picked up the coffeepot and filled both cups, then sat down with his back against the wall. "Care to tell me about it?" he asked, his voice soft, mellowed within the cave.

Blake shrugged and tried to concentrate on the beans. Finally, he tossed the plate aside and pulled the Durham sack from his vest pocket. "I can't talk about it very good, even after all this time," he said, his voice distant while his fingers slowly fashioned a cigarette. "It wasn't an easy thing."

Hank nodded and drew on his cigarette. He waited and smoke drifted lazily from his nostrils.

Blake stared at his cigarette, collecting his thoughts, then he struck a match and inhaled deeply. "They were both dead, Hank. Both Ma and Pa were dead when I got home."

"That's rough, Blake. Sorry don't mean much and helps less, but you've got it."

Blake nodded with a limp smile. "Thanks. You remember when I first met you back in Abilene? A young greenhorn trying to earn five hundred dollars to help his family out?"

Hank smiled slightly with the memory. "Yeah, I do. We had some good times."

Blake stared straight ahead as though he might not have heard Hank's reply. "I changed during that time. Became a man. Killed two men, whored and drank with you, and grew up. But, I never changed as far as my family was concerned. I went home with the money, like I said I would, and was gonna build something nice for the two old people I loved. When I got there, Pa had been dead a year and a half and Ma six months. The ranch was a deserted, broken-down homestead."

"What happened to your brother? I thought he was going

to take care of the place while you were gone. Will is his name, isn't it?"

Blake tried to nod but his head barely moved. "Yeah. It was. I killed him."

Hank's eyes narrowed, but he remained silent. He knew Blake would tell it in the best way he could without questions.

Blake's voice became even softer, as though he were reliving a terrible nightmare. "He killed our ma and pa. Not with a gun or knife, but in a worse way. He quit loving them. And he left them to fend for themselves. Pa died on a bull's horns, and Ma died a year later of a broken heart. Will never came to help them, never saw Pa's grave, and even though Ma was still alive when he came home the last time, he didn't even go in to see her where she was stayin' in town. She died alone in a room above the general store."

"What happened to him, Blake? You thought the world of him when we were on those cattle drives."

"I did. But he changed. Went sour. About six months after I left home, he started going into Smithton, a little town near where we lived. He was drinkin' heavy and trying to act like he was a man. He started running with the Wyler brothers, who are rotten to the very core. It began with rolling drunks, then they went to robbery and murder. I went after them, and it took me two long hard years in the saddle to finally catch up. When I did, it was in Fargo, North Dakota. Will was posing as a rich young businessman from back East. He had the town set up for the taking, with the Wyler brothers as silent partners. I talked to him that last night before I killed him. I asked him about Ma and Pa and why he let them die. He denied it, but I could see he didn't really care one way or the other." Blake closed his eyes and pressed his lips tightly together momentarily. "I killed him the next morning in a legitimate gunfight in the Gold Star saloon."

Hank watched the cold, hard face across from him and he remembered the determined young homesteader he had met the first time four years before. "I'm sorry for you, Blake.

Damned sorry. Whatever happened to those Wylers? Did you ever settle up with them?"

Blake shook his head. "No. I didn't care about them at the time." He looked up and his face brightened slightly with irony. "Funny thing, but I think they're here in Arizona somewhere. I talked with one of the gang members, Todd Andrews, before he was killed in Little Rock Federal Penitentiary. He said the Wylers wintered here in the territory. Close enough to Mexico to sneak across when the heat was on. With Will dead and the gang exposed, I imagine they're sticking pretty close to the border."

"Are you after them?"

"Yes. They're a little unfinished business that kind of hangs over my head. But, I'm not actively looking for them."

Hank waited, giving Blake time to say whatever else might be on his mind. After several silent seconds, he knew there was no more to be said, so he picked up his plate and moved toward the pack in the rear of the cave.

"Speaking of unfinished business, pardner, what say we ride on over and take a little look at our beautiful piece of the desert. The Lady's waitin' for us."

Blake grinned, and he knew it was over and he was glad. "Yeah, might as well. Let's hope she's the only one waiting for us." He moved toward his horse and stopped in the mouth of the cave. "And Hank?"

"Yeah?"

"Thanks for listening."

Hank shrugged. "Nothin' to it. Just a fine art I picked up while waitin' for my neck to be stretched."

## Chapter Five

Hank reined the army mount to a stop and studied the map in his hand. He judged the distance between a bald-faced outcropping of rock, a twisted dead tree and the base of a towering butte.

"Accordin' to this powerful-good map, The Lucky Lady should be waitin' for us on the lee side of that hill just beyond the tree." He sniffed the air and let out a whoop. "Smell that, Blake? Can't ya just smell it?"

Blake tested the air. "Smell what?"

"Silver, son. Pure, beautiful silver."

"Can't smell a damned thing myself."

"Guess you just ain't got the nose for this kind of work," Hank said, with a grin. "I could follow that scent right to that little old mother lode. Come on."

They rode a short distance and Hank pulled up again to stare at a slight depression in the ground on the lee side of the hill. Two feet deep at most, with sloping sides worn smooth by wind and decay, the hole was nothing more than an indentation in the desert.

Hank looked around in wild dismay before jumping from his horse. He ran to a pile of rubble and dug free an old, weathered board which was partially exposed. After brushing the dust from the faded letters, he turned the board to the light. The painted words were barely perceptible, but they had once proudly proclaimed the presence of THE LUCKY LADY MINE.

Blake crossed his hands on the saddle horn and smiled at

the look of disgust on Hank's face. "We find the right piece of nothing?"

"Yeah, guess we did." Hank tossed the sign down with a clatter. "Ain't quite what I expected."

Blake nodded. "Not exactly what I'd call a booming business. And as far as the lady goes, if she was lucky at all she didn't make it this far."

"Now don't get too hasty on me here, Blake. Half of this is yours you know."

"Mine?"

"Yours. I'm givin' it to you to cover your dynamite expenses. A full half."

"Half of what? A hole that isn't even a decent hole?" Blake chuckled and tried to contain a full-fledged laugh. "Tell you what, Hank. How much was in the pot when you won the Lady?"

Wary, Hank looked up. "The hand was worth two thousand bucks. Why?"

"Simple. That makes my half of the Lady worth a thousand. Give me five hundred and you can have the whole thing."

"No way! Half of it's yours, and you ain't gettin' out of it! If I dig, you dig."

"Dig?" Blake asked with a worried glance toward the lowland. "We haven't got time for any digging."

"Sure we do, Blake. We can see for miles from here and if one of us watches while the other . . ."

A small boulder rolled down the hill behind them and Colts were drawn instinctively as they turned toward the sound. A grizzled old prospector walked slowly toward them with his donkey following behind like an obedient pup. Ignoring the drawn weapons, he proceeded down the hill as though he had millenniums to take each step. As he neared, he stopped and brushed his hat back to squint at Blake and Hank.

"You fellers huntin' turkeys with them cannons?"

Remembering the guns, they holstered them and Hank moved toward the miner. "How ya doin', old-timer?"

"Worse'n yestiday'n better'n tommary. Got any tobacco?"

"Sure," Hank said, pulling out the makings and handing them across. "I own The Lucky Lady here," he added proudly.

The prospector rolled a smoke in silence then leaned forward for Hank's offered light. The match singed the old man's long, gray beard, but he seemed not to notice. He nodded and squinted up through the blue haze of smoke. "Ya do, huh? Got a deed?"

Hank smiled broadly as his hand went to his shirt pocket. "Sure have. Right here," he said, handing the paper across. "All legal and proper."

The old-timer took the paper in soiled hands and turned it to the light. His eyes moved over the printing before he handed it back without a change of expression. "Another one of them, huh," he said with a hint of disgust.

"Whatdaya mean, another one of them?"

The old man scratched his head. "Let me recollect here now. Are you the seventh or the eighth? What is it, Maudene?" he asked, turning toward the donkey. "Would you make him the seventh or the eighth?"

The donkey rolled its lips back from yellow teeth and twitched its ears in a massive yawn.

The prospector nodded. "You're right, Maudy. He's the eighth."

"Eighth what?"

"Your bein' here makes you the eighth fool old Larse Larson's 'lost' this mine to. The others put their paper right over there under that rock." He pointed a gnarled finger toward a small boulder. "You'd be just as smart ta do the same."

Blake laughed as he swung down from the saddle and crossed to the boulder. He rolled it aside and picked up the decaying, brown remains of scraps of deeds. He examined two of them closely and could make out the gambler's signature. "This old girl has had quite a few lovers, Hank." He grinned. "Hand me that paper and I'll put your name on file."

"Like hell I will! I can smell it, Blake! It's here, right beneath our feet. All we've gotta do is dig a little bit."

The prospector snorted and swung his arm in a sweeping arc to include all of the expansive desert. "If you're gonna dig here, you might just as well dig anywhere out there. This place ain't no different from the rest of it."

"Yes it is, pop," Hank glowered. "I own this spot."

The prospector smiled a toothless grin. "No you don't, son. Nobody owns the desert or any part of her. She belongs to time. Come on, Maudene. Let's leave fools to fools' work." He moved a few steps and the donkey fell in behind. "Nice lookin' horse," he said as he passed by the cavalry mount.

Hank moved toward the shovel attached to the pack saddle with determined strides, and jerking the spade down, he slammed it into the shallow pit. He dug frantically for several minutes before leaning on the handle to rest. "I gotta try . . . try it, Blake . . . damnit!" he panted. "I at least gotta turn a few shovelfuls."

Blake smiled, but his mind was on the open ground below them. "I really think we should move on, Hank. They're bound to be looking for us."

"I already told ya, we can see anybody for a hundred miles."

"Like we saw that old prospector?"

Hank slammed the shovel into the sandy earth again. "We just wasn't watchin' then. We'll watch now. You take first lookout on that hill and I'll dig. After a bit, we trade off. Deal?"

Blake nodded and pulled his rifle from the saddle scabbard. "Okay, okay. I'm against it, but who can talk sense to a land baron?" He grinned and started up the hill. "But when that trap door goes out from under us, I'm gonna expect an apology on the way down."

"I'll talk fast," Hank returned, bending to his work.

They dug throughout the morning, rested during the heat of the day, and dug again in the cool of evening. The six-foot-square shaft went deeper, and by nightfall Blake was hoisting the dirt high to clear the walls.

"Find anything yet?" Hank called down from his perch high atop the butte.

"Yeah," Blake grunted as he heaved a final spadeful over the side and climbed from the shaft. "Blisters. The old girl is full of 'em."

"Throw 'em back. We want silver and won't settle for anything less," Hank laughed, moving down the hill in the twilight. When he neared, Blake looked at him in disugst.

"What the hell are we looking for anyway, Hank?"

"Silver. Thought you knew that."

"I know that! But what does silver look like? I mean before it winds up on a bartop someplace."

"Haven't got the foggiest. But I'll know when we find some. I'll . . ."

"I know. You'll smell it. That's fine, but for right now I'd like to smell some food cooking. Then, I'd like to get some sleep. And then I'd like to get as far away from that miserable hole in the ground as I can. Let's pull out of here at first light in the mornin'."

"Just till noon, Blake, that's all I ask," Hank pleaded. "If we haven't found anything by noon tomorrow, we'll kiss the old girl good-bye. Deal?"

Blake was too weary to argue.

It was ten o'clock the following day, and as Blake stood guard on the hill his impatience was nearly beyond control. He made up his mind and started down the hill. They were pulling out now and that was all there was to it. He was halfway to the shaft when he heard it, a wild yell originating from somewhere within the bowels of the earth.

"Waaaaaaahooooooo! We hit it! We hit it! Blake! Hey, Blake! Come on down here and give me a hand. We're rich, Blakey boy. Rich beyond your wildest dreams!"

Blake moved into a trot which became a full run. He scrambled to the edge of the pit and looked down at Hank's sweat-streaked face. Hank was seated on the ground and looking up while his hands gently brushed the dust from an odd-shaped boulder still partially embedded in the earth.

"Whatcha got?" Blake asked, the excitement uncontrollable in his voice.

"The smell, boy! The smell! This little mama here is the next thing to pure silver." He patted the rock affectionately. "Your half's still in the ground. Come on down here and help me get it out."

Blake hesitated, then laid the rifle on the edge and dropped into the fledgling shaft. One dug while the other scooped and they pried and tugged and the handle on the shovel broke. Hank dug furiously with the shortened spade and they worked for nearly an hour. The strange rock was coming free now and they both strained to pull it to the level floor of the pit. Several tiny pebbles dropped from above and they froze, staring at each other. Then, slowly, they looked up in unison at the rifles pointing down.

A bearded army sergeant stared down at them in silence, chewed the cud in his cheek, then spat. "Hey, Lieutenant!" he called over his shoulder. "I think we got our boy back. And a horse thief to boot." He leered down and spat again. "If it was up to me, I'd just shoot ya both where ya are and kick a little dirt on top. But I think that might make the captain just a little peeved. He wants ya for himself. So, we'd better take ya on back to the fort. Come on, climb up outta that hole!"

Hank looked at Blake with a weak, apologetic smile. "Got any dynamite left?"

"You miserable jackass, Hank."

"Get on up here before I lose my patience and my hold on this trigger!" the sergeant growled.

Hands reached down roughly and pulled them from the hole. They blinked in the strong sunlight and finally the detachment of cavalry came into focus. And seated behind a private was the old prospector. His donkey stood several feet to the rear.

The lieutenant turned toward the miner. "Well, old-timer, guess you get the reward after all. Glad you found us."

## The Desert Sentinels 39

"When I seed that government brand on that horse, I knowed these two wasn't up to no good. Figgered they'd be a reward. Weren't no trouble findin' ya, either. I know where you patrol in this here desert better'n you do." He looked at Hank and Blake almost sympathetically. "Sorry, fellers. Me and old Maudene there's worked these hills all our lives and never found much to speak of. You're the first real strike we've made. Like I said, sorry."

"I'm sure you are," Hank said acidly. "So sorry it'll take ya at least a week to drink up the reward money. Old bastard."

The sergeant waggled his rifle toward their horses. "You fellers just mount up real easy like. We done took your weapons so all you can do is run. I'd like that 'cause I wouldn't have to take ya back alive. Some of those men you killed were my friends back in the war. I'm feelin' mighty obligated to 'em."

They mounted up, and while their hands were being tied to their saddles, Hank looked across at Blake and winked. "I won't forget that apology, Blake."

"Forget it. I won't be listenin'."

Colonel Nevis Bibby was pleased. Very pleased. And he could fairly see the tree-lined streets of Washington, D.C. With the matter of the outlaw again under control, he could make his plans to hand his command over to Captain Stearns. Bibby poured a drink without caution now and waited for the captain. When a knock came on the door, he called for the captain to enter and poured another drink which he handed to the younger officer.

"Let's drink a toast, Captain," Bibby said, his face glowing. "To your future at Fort Hastings. It's a fine place for a brilliant young officer to further his career."

Stearns nodded his head cordially, but there was a coldness in his eyes that went undetected by the colonel. "Thank you, sir. I welcome this opportunity. Fort Hastings will be a tremendous stepping stone for me and my career. Even greater than you can imagine."

Bibby smiled expansively. "That's the spirit! Now, we have some matters to clear up. First of all, I guess we'll have to go through another bothersome trial . . ."

"Why?"

"Why, what?"

"Excuse me, sir," Stearns said firmly, "but I don't think there is a need for another trial. Lane has already been convicted of murder, and breaking jail is a lesser offense. The other guy was caught red-handed as a horse thief, which automatically is a hanging offense. I say we build a gallows here at the fort, have a military execution and be done with it. You're in command here. You can make that kind of decision."

Bibby hesitated. "Well . . . I . . . I really don't know if that . . ."

"We are an outpost here, sir. And we are our own law. As commanding officer, you will have to stay here to preside over a trial, which means you will miss that boat sailing out of San Francisco for the East Coast in two weeks." Stearns smiled tightly. "Who knows about the military, sir? In that length of time they may well change their mind and send me to another assignment."

Bibby nearly choked on his whiskey. "No, by God! I've been in this stinking . . . I, ah, I mean, I've served here as long as I can . . . ah, hem, I . . . I've been here a long time. I think you're absolutely right. We'll have a summary court. I'll preside. You set the quartermaster to the task of building a gallows. Better yet, have the one in town torn down and hauled out here. We paid for the damned thing anyway. Say, in two days from now we'll do what must be done and be through with it."

"Very wise decision, sir. The Arizona Territory is still under military rule. We are within our jurisdiction. The civilians screwed it up last time, now it's the army's turn to do it right."

"Absolutely. Now, there is another slight matter that might come to some difficulty. As you know, the wagon that was stolen contained three hundred rifles which were to be passed along for a paltry sum to a Mexican named Juárez. His emissary is due here within the next few days, and I'd say he won't be exactly pleased when he finds out we have no rifles to give him. This matter will have to be handled very delicately, and I would appreciate your assistance at the proper time."

Stearns bowed stiffly from the waist. "My pleasure, sir. If you don't mind my saying so, I think it is a grievous mistake for the United States to be selling weapons to a revolutionary band of rabble."

Bibby smiled again, and he knew he liked the young captain. "My sentiments exactly, Captain Stearns. I can see we think alike. Two great military minds with a single purpose. Perhaps one day I will have the pleasure of having you serve under my command."

Stearns gazed at the colonel with glazed eyes which hid his utter contempt. "It would be my pleasure, sir. If you will excuse me now, there are many things to do."

"Certainly, Captain. Feel free to drop in if there is anything you need help with."

Stearns saluted briskly, to which Bibby waved his hand, and spun on his heel and left. Bibby poured another stiff shot, then went to his living quarters in the rear of the building to try on his dress uniform.

Blake heard the pounding and hammering and laid an ear against the wall of the windowless cell. He watched Hank lying on his cot, eyes closed, as he listened. "What do you think they're building, Hank?"

"It's not a squirrel cage."

"They wouldn't do it that quick, would they? I mean, we haven't even had a trial yet."

Hank opened one eye. "I already had a trial, if you could call it that." He closed the eye again. "As for you, they don't try horse thieves. Never mind tellin' 'em you just borrowed it."

Blake eased onto the other cot and clasped his hands behind his head to stare at the log ceiling of the stockade. The silence in the small cell was interrupted only by a muffled thumping of hammers on wood.

"Sorry I got you into this mess, Blake," Hank said softly, without looking across.

Blake laughed nervously and swung his feet over the edge of the cot. "Forget it, Hank. You didn't get me into it. I got myself in."

"Like hell. If I hadn't been so damned stupid about that mine, we could have gotten away. Had the fever, I guess. Like holdin' four aces with only a dollar to bet."

"When you said you'd hit it, I damned near broke my leg runnin' down that hill, and I would've kept going too, even if it was broke. I think you could say that's a little more than a casual interest."

Hank chuckled. "Would've been somethin', wouldn't it?"

"Sure would've. Hank? Do you think that last boulder really did have some silver in it?"

"Naw. Just another stupid, ugly, heavy rock."

Metal clanged against metal and they heard the draw bar on the door being pulled to one side. An iron key stabbed at the lock and Blake's eyes darted to the tiny hole on their side. "Whatcha think they want?" he asked on hissing breath.

"They're comin' to tell you you're guilty. Of course, you'll have to stand before the colonel to hear that, after they've had their little laugh over your trial. See you in about fifteen minutes."

The door swung open on protestisng hinges and two armed soldiers were framed in the doorway. "Which one of you is the horse thief?" the shorter man asked.

"Neither of us," Hank replied flatly. "Try the next cell."

The tall soldier stepped part way inside. "Don't give us any of your guff, fella. Come on," he said, stabbing a finger at Blake. "The colonel and the captain are gonna preside over your trial."

Blake hunched wearily to his feet and glanced at Hank. "What's preside mean, Hank?"

"That's army talk for finding out who's the best liar. I'll lay five on Stearns."

Blake grinned as he was shoved roughly through the door.

Fifteen minutes later, the door swung open again and Blake was pushed inside. He shook his head in disbelief and sank to the edge of his cot. Hank sat up, yawned, then leaned forward to rest his elbows on his knees. "How'd it go?"

"I can't believe it, Hank. They really are going to hang us!"

"Kinda thought that's what they had in mind. What did they say at your, for want of a better word, trial?"

"Well, after I said not guilty, they kinda left me out of the conversation. That miserable old prospector was there . . ."

"Waiting for his reward."

". . . and the sergeant who arrested us at the mine, along with Stearns and the colonel and the guy I bought the dynamite from. They all identified me like I was the prize apple pie at a bake-off. I didn't win any ribbons, but they did say they'd give me a necktie."

"When?"

"As soon as they finish buildin' the damned thing."

Hank moved to the wall and listened. The pounding and sawing had stopped. He spun away from the wall. "They can't do that! What about that last supper stuff, huh? And sunrise?" he added quickly as though there might be hope. "They're supposed to do that at sunrise, by God! Not in the heat of the day!"

Blake smiled indulgently. "I think they're using the rule book for a door stop. Seem to be in a pretty anxious hurry to get this over with."

"But what about us, damnit! Maybe we ain't in such a goddamned awful big rush! Steak and potatoes sounds pretty damned good to me right about now."

Blake leaned back. Somehow, Hank's consternation relieved his own anxiety. "Well, Hank, old buddy, I don't think you're gonna have to worry about picking your teeth. They were throwing the rope over when I came back." Blake paused, studying his friend. "I got you out of the last one, if you remember. I think it's your turn."

"Yeah, but you happened to be on the *outside* at the time, if you remember. I'm workin' with a little bigger handicap." Hank ran his hands through his hair and sank to the edge of his cot. "Never mind. I'll think of something."

"I hope you do. And mighty quick."

## Chapter Six

Rodrigo reined the big stallion in and the riders behind moved up to form a line one hundred yards in front of Fort Hastings' main gate. He studied the rifles leveled at them over the wall and knew the ten-pound cannon was being rolled into position. A closing hatred seeped into the corners of his mind, the same hatred he always felt when in the presence of regular military. He had already told his men to beware of treachery, and eleven pairs of dark eyes watched the thick walls with sullen distrust. The single pair of blue eyes watched as well, but with humorous disconcern. Rodrigo nudged his horse and moved forward alone toward the gates.

A burly sergeant loomed atop the wall and trained his Spencer on Rodrigo's chest. "Halt! State your name and mission!"

Rodrigo touched the reins and the horse stopped. A smile flashed on his dark face and white teeth were made even whiter in the field of brown. "Rodrigo's my name. I am here to discuss a business matter. I represent Benito Pablo Juárez, and I wish to speak with Colonel Nevis Bibby."

The sergeant hesitated before quitting the wall. Minutes later, the gates swung open and Rodrigo motioned for his men to move up beside him.

"Beware," he said in Spanish as they entered the fort. "Groups of three in three corners, weapons ready but not drawn. If we must fight, wait for my signal. Biggie, you and Cassildo wait outside the colonel's office with the pack animals."

They were inside the fort now and the gates closed behind

them. The groups moved casually to their stations and Rodrigo stepped down before the headquarters building. Seeing the gallows off to one side, a tinge of revulsion twisted his stomach. He was met by Corporal Darby standing beside the door, who started to salute then thought better of it.

Rodrigo looked at the corporal and stared through him. "I'm here to see the colonel."

Corporal Darby held his rifle in one hand before his chest and rapped on the door with the knuckles of the other. "Someone to see you, sir!"

"Send him in."

Opening the door, Darby stood to one side and Rodrigo nodded as he stepped inside.

Colonel Bibby scrambled to his feet with as much flourish as his bulk would allow and crossed the room with hand extended. Captain Stearns stood to one side and his cold eyes met with Rodrigo's. Rodrigo's eyes never wavered and he knew immediately that he did not like the man.

"Pleased to meet you, sir," Bibby gushed, reaching for Rodrigo's slowly rising hand. "I'm Colonel Bibby."

Rodrigo's sombrero dipped slightly as he gripped soft flesh. "Rodrigo."

"It's an honor to have you here, Rodrigo," Bibby said, pulling his hand back and flexing his fingers before indicating Captain Stearns. "And this is Captain Mathew Stearns. The new commandant of Fort Hastings."

Rodrigo nodded, and Stearns matched it curtly.

Bibby bustled toward the whiskey bottle and filled two glasses, then held it over a third with a glance toward the captain. Stearns shook his head. Bibby shrugged and added a topping to his own glass. He handed a glass to Rodrigo, now leaning against the desk with ankles crossed but his revolver and knife were hanging free for immediate use.

"To your health, sir," Bibby exulted, "and to the well-being and continued friendship of our two magnificent countries."

Rodrigo extended his glass toward the colonel's before taking a small drink. The colonel's glass was nearly a quarter down when he lowered it from his lips.

"Can we talk?" Rodrigo asked, his eyes locked on Stearns' face once again. Stearns stiffened visibly, but Bibby didn't notice.

"Of course we can. What was it that you wanted to see me about?"

Rodrigo's dark, fathomless eyes fell upon the colonel. Bibby tried to smile, and his lips twitched as he nervously raised the glass again.

"Rifles," Rodrigo said simply.

Bibby continued to struggle with his smile and continued to fail. "Rifles? What rifles?"

"Three hundred Spencer repeaters, caliber thirty, which your government agreed to sell to Benito Pablo Juárez."

"Oh, those rifles," Bibby managed, giving up on the smile completely. "I'm terribly sorry, Mr. Rodrigo, but I'm afraid we will not be able to live up to the terms of our agreement."

Rodrigo's eyes narrowed. "I am not a patient man, Colonel. I have the specified amount of American currency, and I am here for the rifles."

"I'm sure you have. Yes, I'm sure you do," Bibby said, his red face taking on an even deeper shade. His jowls quivered and he pressed his knuckles behind his back in a well-practiced military maneuver while turning to pace the room. Then he turned with an apologetic, weak grin. "But we do not have the rifles."

"Explain."

"Well . . . ah . . . hem . . . yes. Certainly. We owe you that much. The detachment which was sent to protect the shipment was ambushed. Dreadful thing. Sixteen troopers killed and the wagon confiscated."

"Who was in command?"

"Why, Captain Stearns here, as a matter of fact. He was coming out from back East to take over . . ."

Rodrigo's gaze shifted to Stearns. "What happened?"

"We were overpowered," Stearns said, with a shrug. "At

least thirty men. To save what was left of my command, I had to surrender the weapons."

"Who were they?"

"We don't know for sure. But, we did capture two of them. They are in the stockade right now awaiting their punishment."

"I'll talk to them," Rodrigo said icily, placing the nearly full glass on the desk top.

Stearns straightened and his words were equally cold. "That won't be necessary. They have been asked questions at length and will not co-operate. They are to be hanged by the neck until dead."

A bemused smile crossed Rodrigo's face. "And that, Captain, is intended to help their speaking ability? I'd rather talk to them *before* their necks are broken."

"I've already told you," Stearns said, the heat rising in his voice, "they will not talk. And neither you, nor any other representative of a foreign government is going to interrogate United States prisoners."

The humor faded in Rodrigo's eyes and the cold deadliness returned. "Why do you insist that I not speak with them?"

Bibby bustled up but stood cautiously to one side. "Yes, Captain. Why not let the man talk with them? He might be able . . ."

"Because I am in command here now, Colonel! We handled that little matter this morning, did we not? If you wish to pull rank on me, that's fine. But, if you do, I'll petition for a full inquiry into your competence and judgment in the field. You will be retained here until that inquest is completed."

Bibby blanched and gulped the whiskey before wiping trembling lips with the back of a pudgy hand. "That won't be necessary, Captain. Of course, you are absolutely correct. My apologies." He turned to face Rodrigo. "I am terribly sorry, Mr. Rodrigo, but your speaking with the prisoners is entirely out of the question."

Rodrigo watched both men as he straightened to his full height. "As you wish, gentlemen. At what time can I expect delivery of the next shipment of rifles?" He looked directly at Stearns. "And, delivered into my hands this time, Captain."

Stearns bristled at the rebuke. "That is a matter you will have to take up with the War Department, sir. I haven't the authority . . ."

"I know how much authority you have, Captain," Rodrigo said with a casual smile. "More than you can handle, I suspect. And as for your War Department, I arranged the previous shipment with them, and I don't have another six months to wait."

Stearns returned the smile without humor. "I'd say that's your problem. Go through channels or go elsewhere." He glanced at the clock on the wall. "If you will excuse us now, we have some military business to conduct precisely at twelve noon. Colonel? The prisoners should be crossing the parade ground at any moment now. If you will excuse me, I will go and do my duty."

"Certainly, Captain," Bibby said, returning Stearns' crisp salute with a desultory wave of the hand while edging closer to Rodrigo. "Personally, Mr. Rodrigo, I wish things had worked out differently for you. But, as they haven't, would you please stay as my guest for the execution? I've never seen one before, and I'll admit I'm a little more than curious. Then we'll have lunch."

"Thank you, but no, Colonel. I find no pleasure in watching men die. Especially at the end of a rope."

They were on the front porch now, and they stopped to watch two men, hands bound behind their backs, being escorted by a squad of soldiers toward the waiting platform.

Blake walked behind Hank, linked to him by the chain around their waists. He edged up closer.

"Come up with anything yet, Hank," he asked in a hoarse whisper.

"Nope. But I'm still workin' on it."

"That's good. Real good, and comforting as hell. But either

you'd better start working faster or we'd better start walking slower. I think we're running out of time."

"Goddamnit, Blake!" Hank hissed in return. "If I walk any slower we'll be backing up. But, let's give it a try anyway."

Their pace slowed noticeably, and a soldier in the rear shoved Blake's shoulder. "Move it along, gunner. We ain't got all day."

"He's worried about time, Hank," Blake said, picking up the pace again. "Says he hasn't got all day."

"Poor bastard," Hank mumbled. "I think we're the ones with the real time problem around here."

They mounted the thirteen stairs and were led to stand before twin nooses dangling from the crossbeam. A sergeant stood before them with two sacks in his hand and he raised them nonchalantly.

"With or without?"

"We aren't ordering a drink here, pal," Hank said acidly. "We've got nothin' to hide from anybody. I'll go down with the sun on my face, and I want to be turned in the other direction. I want to watch those bastards watch an innocent man hang."

The sergeant shrugged. "Suit yourself, it ain't gonna make the rope any longer. Any last words?"

"Yeah. Your mother sure had ugly babies."

Rodrigo watched the backs of the two men standing before the ropes and the hatred boiled in his heart. He had seen that too many times in Argentina, and had stood before the rope himself. He turned away and began adjusting the cinch strap on the pack saddle.

Biggie Munn watched the proceeding with apathetic disconcern. Then his blue eyes hardened and his mouth dropped open slightly as Hank and Blake were turned to face the crowd. The ropes were around their necks now and they were standing squarely over the trap doors. A private stood with his hand on the trip lever, watching Captain Stearns and waiting for the signal.

A choking gurgle came from Munn's muted mouth, and he

lashed the rowels into his horse's sides while his hand snatched the bola from the saddle horn. The horse was instantly into a gallop and the three hard balls whirled around Munn's head. A shout went up from the soldiers and Colonel Bibby gasped in shock. The bola sailed at lightning speed and Rodrigo looked up to see the thongs tear into the private's neck, twirl, lift him off his feet and slam him to the ground with his hand trailing over the lever.

"*Companieros!*" Rodrigo screamed and the knife flashed from his hip, its tip finding the soft flesh under Colonel Bibby's second chin. The ten riders raised their rifles simultaneously with some of them aimed at Captain Stearns, others trained on the soldiers collected in the parade ground.

Munn leaped from his horse with incredible grace for a man so huge and bounded up the stairs. His knife was in his hand and sharp metal slashed through hemp effortlessly.

Hank grinned and pulled the noose from his neck. "Howdy, Big. Glad you could make it." He turned to Blake. "Told you I'd figure something out. Nothing to it. Piece of cake."

Ignoring Hank's remark, Blake stepped quickly off the trap door and grasped Biggie Munn's hand at the same time. "Thank God for you, Biggie! You're the most beautiful person I've seen in my entire life!"

Munn threw his head back and laughed hugely, and for the first time, Blake didn't notice the wagging stump or hear the sickening gurgle.

"Let's get off this sonofabitch," Hank said with a cautious glance around. "A man could get killed up here."

Rodrigo's knife point drew a tiny trickle of blood from Bibby's neck as the colonel jerked and quivered. "What . . . what's the meaning of this? I'll have you . . . have you . . . arrested for . . . for treason, by God! I'm . . ."

"Sorry, Colonel, but your party's over. Those two men are friends of mine, and whatever they're charged with, I give you my guarantee that they are innocent. Now, order one of your men to get their weapons and mounts. And get a horse for the captain as well."

Bibby's florid face bulged over his neckline. "No, by God! I'm in command here and I . . ."

The knife point pricked his flesh more deeply. "Do it. The only thing you're in command of right now is your ability to remain alive. We will be taking the captain with us for a distance. You can be in command until he gets back. Now do as instructed!"

The colonel managed to blurt some orders to his corporal and the soldier ran toward the stables while Hank, Blake and Biggie Munn neared. Rodrigo looked them in the eye and his face was hard.

"Did you do it?" he asked without emotion.

Hank's hands flew up in exasperation. "Hell no, we didn't do it, Rod!"

Rodrigo nodded. "That's good enough for me. Good to see you again, Blake. Hank."

"It's not half as good as seeing you, Rod. And Munn here," Blake said. "All I can do is say thanks."

"No thanks necessary." Rodrigo nodded toward the horses being led across the parade ground. "Get your weapons and horses. Captain!" he shouted to the stock-still officer, "you mount up as well. You'll ride with us. Once you and my men are clear of the fort, I'll release the colonel. Blake, you stay with me. Biggie? If we don't catch up in five minutes, kill him."

The captain swung up and jerked the horse's head around viciously. As if upon cue, the revolutionaries moved up and closed about the captain. With Biggie Munn in the lead, they cantered through the opening gates. When they were out of rifle range, Rodrigo withdrew the knife from Bibby's throat. "Thank you for your hospitality, Colonel," he said, as he and Blake stepped into their saddles. "We'll meet again some day I'm sure."

"You're . . . damned . . . right we will!" Bibby spluttered. "And when we do, I'll see you hang, by God!"

Rodrigo turned in the saddle and smiled down pleasantly.

"You're quite taken with that pastime, Colonel. But remember, the noose fits all necks. Even yours."

Rodrigo touched his horse lightly with the rowels and Blake followed with the packhorse on lead. A detachment of mounted cavalry were approaching from an oblique angle, and they could see that Captain Stearns had waved the troop away. Rodrigo touched the brim of his hat as they passed, and Blake glanced at the soldiers for a moment as they neared. Then his head jerked around and he stared at the big sergeant leading the patrol and watched his back until they passed into the fort and out of sight. He was puzzled. He knew he had seen that face somewhere before.

## Chapter Seven

They were fifty miles from the border and bathed in brilliant moonlight when Rodrigo pulled in his mount. He had talked to neither Blake nor Hank during the entire ride and they were silent now as they watched him hand the officer's revolver and saber across.

"I'd like to say it's been pleasant, Captain," Rodrigo said as Stearns buckled on the sword and slammed his revolver into its holster, "but it hasn't."

"You'll wear my steel one day," Stearns replied, lips drawn tight and eyes cold. "And you'll wear it through your stomach and out your back."

Rodrigo smiled pleasantly. "Knowing you, Captain, I suspect it would be the other way around. Through the back and out the stomach?" He turned and gazed south, into the land that was Mexico beyond. "Have you ever been to Mexico, Captain Stearns. Nogales, perhaps?"

"No. And I don't plan to change that."

"You should, one day. It is a beautiful land, with beautiful people. Kind, gentle people. But, unfortunately, there is a corrupt government and an equally corrupt military. They hang innocent men for their own purposes. Much like in your country."

Stearns held the reins tight and the horse backed against the pressure of the bit. "Can I go now?" he demanded.

Rodrigo watched the horse fighting the hard steel against its jaw. "Certainly. But, please, be more gentle with the horse. It will serve a kind master as well as a cruel one."

"I don't need your advice on how to ride a horse," Stearns

snarled. "Nor on the virtues of a hangman's noose." He slammed his tiny spurs into the horse's flanks and it bolted north at a dead run.

Rodrigo shook his head sadly as the horse and rider disappeared into the night shadows. Then his gaze drifted to Hank and Blake. He watched them silently for long seconds before allowing a smile to spread across his face.

"Hello, my two wayward friends. How did you manage to get your necks so close to the hangman's noose?"

Both Hank and Blake opened their mouths to speak, but Rodrigo silenced them with a friendly wave of his hand. "On second thought, I'd better hear this over a tequila. Knowing you two from the drives, that might be advisable."

The sun was breaking across the flat, mesquite-splattered land as their horses stepped into the murky waters of the Rio Grande. Blake looked down at the shallow water and a strange sensation came over him which he could not explain. Here he was, crossing into a foreign land, a fugitive on the run. But there was something exhilarating about it, an excitement he had never experienced before. Is this how Will felt, he wondered, riding carefree with the Wyler brothers? They probably crossed into Mexico many times in situations similar to this. Was he wrong for . . .

"We're in Mexico now, Blake," Hank said, moving his horse alongside. "The middle of this river is the boundary. Seems a little strange, doesn't it? On one side of the river they speak Mexican, and on the other they speak English. The President of the country on one bank ain't nothin' but an ordinary man on the other."

They were clattering from the stream bed now and Blake nodded his agreement. "I was just thinking about that. Or something like it." He looked ahead and saw Rodrigo, relaxed in the saddle but yet commanding. "Old Rod hasn't had much to say to us, has he?"

"No, he's that way. If something needs to be said, he'll say it. If not, he's pretty tight with the words."

"Where we headed anyway?"

"I don't know, but from the direction we're going, my guess would be Cananea. I really don't give a damn where it is though, long as my back's to that river and there's a southern breeze on my face."

"How long do you think we should stay here?"

"Long enough to give those boys back at the fort something else to think about." A look of wistful remembrance came into Hank's eyes. "I spent some time in Cananea two winters ago and I know a little lass there worth losing a little sleep over. Her name's Constance and her twin sister's called Maria. A couple of beauties, they. And friendly. Very friendly. If that's where we're headed, I don't think you'll regret spending a week or two in Mexico. Then I'd like to angle northeast. I've got some business to take up with a gambler in New Orleans."

Blake grinned. "What kind of business?"

"I've got a deed to a silver mine, and I think I might like to lose it in a poker game."

"I've got a blister or two I'd like to present to him myself."

"Deal then?" Hank asked. "After a few days here, New Orleans? You ain't gonna believe that town, Blake old boy. Cajuns they call the ladies there. Part French and part Creole. Never seen nothing to match that cross breedin' for comin' up with pretty."

"Got nowhere else to go," Blake laughed. "Might as well have a look for myself."

The cobbled streets of Cananea still smelled of musty water from the afternoon sprinkling, and the plaza was deserted. Whitewashed adobe walls reflected the sun's strong glare, and the shade of the trees surrounding the square looked cool and inviting. The clatter of shod hooves on cobblestone rattled through the maze of alleyways leading to the plaza and echoed off silent buildings. Rodrigo angled toward the veranda of an apparently deserted *cantina* and eased gracefully from the saddle. When their horses were tied to the rail, he turned toward Hank and Blake and threw his arms wide and embraced them with warm affection.

"Welcome to Mexico, Hank, Blake. This is my second home. In many ways, it reminds me much of Argentina."

Blake returned the powerful embrace, as did Hank. Then he gazed around, searching for some sign of life. "Where is everybody, Rod? The place looks abandoned."

"Siesta time, Blake my friend. Siesta time. Everyone, no matter what their station in life, sleeps in the heat of the afternoon. A very healthy custom. But, come," Rodrigo said, with a sweeping gesture of his hand toward the doorway, "Señor Rosallio has slept long enough. We are hungry and thirsty, and there is much to talk about."

Their heavy Mexican rowels jangled as the riders stepped onto the packed earthen floor of the *cantina*. It too had been swept and sprinkled and the smell of meat being simmered slowly brought a growl to Blake's stomach. The riders approached the bar and the Mexicans talked excitedly among themselves while Rodrigo, Munn, Hank and Blake moved as a group to one side. Rodrigo smacked his palm against the bar and shouted in strong Spanish, "Hola, Rosallio! We are thirsty and hungry *vaqueros* down here! You have slept long enough! Give the bed to your wife and children and come earn your living for a change!"

Grumbling came from the winding adobe staircase and presently a small, nearly bald man scurried into the room, tucking his white shirt into matching pants as he moved. He saw Rodrigo and his face glowed with pleasure.

"Ah, Señor Rodrigo! You have returned safely. We thank the Son of God for this favor."

Rodrigo smiled kindly. "Thank you, Rosallio. And thank him for us in your prayers. Please, meet two American friends of mine. Blake Evans and Hank Lane."

The proprietor shook hands agreeably before turning to shout playful obscenities at the Mexicans while his hands went quickly for the tequila bottle and glasses. When all were filled, he retrieved two bowls of cut limes from beneath the counter and two shakers of salt.

Blake watched curiously as the Mexicans lapped wrist with

tongue, sprinkled the moistened spot with salt, gulped the tequila, licked the salt and then devoured the lime.

Hank watched Blake in his confusion. "That's the way they do it around here," he said, moistening his wrist and sprinkling salt. "Seems like drinkin' whiskey is a hell of a lot easier, but this always gets the job done just the same. Try it."

Blake licked his wrist, applied the salt and downed the tequila. All eyes watched, waiting for his reaction. Two ounces of white fire scorched a trail down his throat, he nearly choked on the lime and his eyes watered as he chewed the last of the bitter fruit. "That's potent stuff," he finally managed. "Don't know which is worse, the tequila or that green thing."

Rodrigo clapped him between the shoulder blades. "That green thing is a lime. I think you might live longer on those than the tequila. Perhaps we will know by morning."

"Señor Rosallio, may I see that bottle please?" Hank asked, astounding Blake with his mastery of Spanish.

The patron nodded and handed an unopened bottle across before filling the glasses again. Holding the bottle up to the light, Hank studied it before placing it on the bar with a satisfied smile. "Take a look, Blake," he said off-handedly.

Curious, Blake turned the bottle to the light and his stomach turned in the same instant. Lying on the bottom, apparently dead, was a wrinkled, ugly-white insect that resembled a grub worm. He could feel the lime and tequila rising and swallowed hard to keep it in place.

"What is a bug doing in there?"

"Shhhhh," Hank said, pressing a finger to his lips. "Poor little feller's passed out."

Rodrigo and Munn laughed heartily, then Rodrigo translated for the others and they howled with delight. A full glass was before Blake again now and he fingered the drink gingerly with a cautious glance into the tequila.

Hank nudged Blake's ribs gently. "Let me give you a little advice, Blake old buddy. Don't ever take a look at an apple after the second bite."

Blake grinned, salted his wrist and downed the drink. "That's good advice, Hank," he said, chewing on his lime, "but a guy's a damned fool not to look at it before he takes that first one."

While dinner was being prepared, the four of them retired to a table, each with a bottle of Mexican beer. Rodrigo laid his sombrero carefully on a nearby table and ran his hands through his jet-black hair. He toasted Hank and Blake again before taking a long, thirsty swallow from the bottle. "I think I'm prepared for this now," he said, lowering the bottle and leaning back in his chair. "What happened back at Fort Hastings?"

"I'm the one at fault, I guess," Hank began. "I won a silver mine in a poker game in New Orleans . . ."

"That figures."

"Thanks, Rod. Anyway, I was going there to work the mine. Went to sleep in a nearby cave and the next thing I knew, Stearns was draggin' me out by my ankles. Said I'd ambushed his troops, took his wagon and that he would see to it personal like that I got hung. I'd never seen him or his troops before, but there was no telling him that. He was as convinced as a bear with a pawful of honey that he'd found the right tree. So, I was tried, convicted and condemned. The night before I was supposed to hang, old Blake here sneaks into town, blows up half the jail, and we ride north. With me ridin' a stolen, excuse me, Blake, a *borrowed* government horse. To make a long story short, we stopped for a peek at the mine, they caught us and took both of us back to hang. Then you showed up, thank Christ."

Rodrigo nodded and his eyes shifted. "Blake?"

"My story's about the same as Hank's. I found out in Abilene that Hank had gone to Arizona. When I got to Twin Buttes, I saw the gallows and knew somebody was about to play his last hand. Little'd I know it was old Hank here. When I did find out, I bought some dynamite, blew the wall out of the jail house . . ."

"And me damned near as well."

"... *confiscated* a horse that, unfortunately, was wearing an army brand. Next thing to tell is how glad I was to see Biggie's beautiful mug starin' at me on that hangin' platform."

Rodrigo nodded and raised the bottle again.

"How about you and Big, Rod?" Hank asked. "How'd you happen to show up there?"

Rodrigo smiled tersely. "To pick up the rifles that you were supposed to have stolen."

Hank and Blake looked at each other. "Rifles? What rifles?" they asked in unison.

"They didn't tell you at your supposed trial, Hank?" Rodrigo observed with no question intended. "I thought not. But that's really what you were being hanged for. The theft of three hundred Spencer, five-shot repeater, thirty-caliber rifles. And ten thousand rounds of ammunition."

Rodrigo paused to roll a cigarette and as flame touched paper, he looked at Hank again. "You're certain there was no mention of what was in the wagon?"

"None."

"And Stearns positively identified you as having been leader of those who ambushed the detachment?"

"Without blinking an eye, the lying bastard."

Rodrigo drew on the cigarette before speaking again. "You were sentenced to hang for having participated in the killing of sixteen troopers, but isn't it interesting why no one ever questioned why a roving outlaw band would encumber themselves with something as slow and heavy as a meaningless supply wagon, the tracks of which mysteriously disappear?"

Blake listened to Rodrigo's words and marveled at the keen, probing precision of his mind. He knew that the man of the cold eyes across from him had been a wealthy, educated man in his Argentinian homeland, and he wondered what his calling had been. Then his mind caught up with the conversation and he nodded in agreement with Hank and Munn that, yes, it was indeed strange.

"It's not strange at all," Rodrigo said, signaling for more drinks. "The killing of those troopers, sixteen men slain in ambush, was sufficient to inflame public sentiment against you. The testimony of a respected cavalry officer was sufficient evidence. But, in point of fact, you were not sentenced to be hanged for murder. You were to be hanged to ensure your eternal silence."

Confused, Hank shook his head. "I'm not sure I understand everything about what you're saying, Rod. All I know is that I didn't do it, and according to my country logic, that means somebody else did." He grinned and reached for the fresh beer. "Ain't I a dazzler with the mental footwork?"

Rodrigo and Munn laughed, but Blake continued to watch Rodrigo's face. "Do you know who did it, Rod?"

Rodrigo nodded.

"Who?"

Now the Argentinian smiled. "All in good time, Blake. All in good time. I'd like to give it more thought."

"Well, while old Rod's thinkin' about that," Hank said, pushing away from the table, "I've got other things to think about. Come on, Blake. I think Connie and Maria might be up from their afternoon snooze by now."

Blake started to rise, but stopped when Rodrigo spoke again.

"Blake, do you have a moment? I'd like to speak with you alone."

"Sure, Rod," Blake said, sinking down again. "See you later, Hank."

Hank shrugged and motioned to Munn. "Come on, Big, I'll buy you a drink." The huge man grinned, glanced at Rodrigo, who nodded, and stood. "I like drinkin' with Biggie," Hank continued with a laugh. "Don't have to listen to his troubles." He clapped a massive shoulder and they turned away.

Rodrigo poured two glasses of tequila and spoke while he salted his wrist. "Why aren't you with your family?"

Blake hesitated and looked down before speaking.

"Because I haven't got a family. They're all dead."

Rodrigo's eyes never wavered, showed no change of emotion. "How?"

Blake retold the story and Rodrigo listened as a father might to a troubled son. When Blake finished telling of his parents and how he had killed his brother, he fell silent, watching the man on the other side of the table. "You knew that would happen, Rod," he said, his voice a stilled whisper. "You warned me. How did you know?"

"I didn't know."

"Yes you did, in a way. That night on the trail, you said I should go home, take care of my family. I disagreed, saying my brother would take care of them and that I needed money to do what I wanted to do for them. And you said, 'Yes, Blake, but who is taking care of your brother?' I remember your words exactly. It's like you knew, like you were warning me. What I can't understand is how did you know?"

Rodrigo chewed his lime thoughtfully for long moments, and when he finished, there was a warm, understanding smile on his face. "First, let me say how deeply saddened I am by your tragedy. It is a terrible thing, and the feeling of emptiness is nearly unbearable. I lost my entire family in a similar manner, as did Munn. And Hank? Perhaps it was worse for him than the rest of us. He never had a family. I know what such a loss does to the heart and soul. It congeals the blood of the mind into a coursing stream of hatred. And rage. You were right to kill your brother."

The dark face became contemplative and hard eyes stared into clear tequila.

"Money corrupts, Blake, but a lack of money is equally corruptive. You were corrupted, to a certain degree, by life on the trail with men whose future has been swallowed by the past. When I first met you, you were a homesteader. When I last saw you, you had killed two men—none by choice I agree —slept in scented beds and drunk with carefree men trapped in their life of indifference."

The eyes were on Blake now and there was a philosophical depth to them. "Contrary to your belief, I didn't know what would happen to you when you got home. I only knew that you would not be the same when you got home. Hence, home would not be the same. Younger brothers are seldom strong; their mental strength is sapped by sibling rivalry. My warning to you about your brother, younger by two years as I recall, was merely an extension of my own experience. I am truly sorry I had to be correct in my assumption."

Blake silently digested the depth and meaning of the words he had just heard while his fingers slowly turned the glass before him.

Rodrigo watched him patiently, and when he spoke there was a soft finality in his tone. "There were three gauchos on our last drive, Blake. Biggie Munn, Hank Lane and myself. Men who have no ties except those that bind them to what is right, as opposed to the easier choice, that which is wrong. Men who live by their wits, men of the plains who guide their destiny on a course set only by the stars. In the main, they are gentle men. But when the congealed bloodstream of hatred flows, the inner rage is irrepressible. You are now the fourth gaucho. And I give you my hand."

Rodrigo reached across the table, and Blake watched the lean brown hand momentarily. Then he grasped it firmly and they shook as men will who care about each other. When their hands withdrew, Rodrigo looked toward the window to check the position of the sun before again pouring from the tequila bottle.

"I must meet with Benito at sunset. Would you care to join me? It would be good for you to live the experience of being in the company of a great and compassionate man. Such a combination is seldom found in mankind."

Blake shrugged weakly. "Sure, Rod. I'd like to meet him, if it's all right."

"If it weren't all right, I wouldn't have invited you." Rodrigo paused to drink and study his mind. "Strangely, it is our war against the French, and their puppet, Maximilian, that nearly got you and Hank hung. The United States is attempting to avoid direct intervention into our war against the French who are presently making a colonial incursion into Mexico. But, a strong French presence on their southern border is not to their liking, so they have agreed to sell us desperately needed weapons to win the conflict. That shipment which, unfortunately, crossed your trail, was to have been a godsend. We need those weapons if we are to win. Those that we have now are antiquated, single-shot rifles which, often as not, misfire." Rodrigo smiled bitterly. "But, we do not have them, do we?"

Blake shook his head. "Does Juárez know the rifles were stolen?"

"Yes. I informed him by courier. We must decide tonight what course we are to follow."

"How did you meet Juárez in the first place?"

"I was educated as a barrister, a lawyer, in my country as a youth. Spending my life in a courtroom never appealed to me and, much to my father's dismay, I chose a life on the pampas —our plains—instead. We had large cattle holdings, and it was necessary that one of the sons become involved in the business. My father and I traveled to Mexico City one summer to arrange the sale of some cattle. It was there that I met Benito, who was also schooled as a lawyer, and a friendship developed that has endured these many long years."

"Are you involved in this war strictly because of friendship?" Blake asked, sprinkling salt on his wrist.

"That, and two other reasons. First, I believe in my friend Benito. He is called, 'The Mexican Washington,' in reference to your great leader. As minister of justice, Benito issued the 'Ley Juárez,' which was a reform measure abolishing the special courts, the kind of courts which sentenced you and Hank to the gallows, and reduced the power of the army and the church. He is a man of the people, a great libertarian. And secondly, once we have defeated the French, Benito has agreed to help me initiate a revolution in my own country to win Argentina back from the corrupt jackals who are now in power."

Rodrigo paused and gazed across the room now flooded by twilight. A different depth came into his eyes and they resembled twin pits of molten passion. "That is the only thing I live for," he said softly, "and the thing for which I would gladly die."

Overwhelmed by the strength and dedication of the man across from him, Blake sipped his drink and allowed Rodrigo's words to be absorbed by silent adobe walls and thick wooden beams. Rodrigo seemed content to gaze, lost in a reverie of thought. Finally, Blake rolled a cigarette and leaned back.

"I've been thinking about what you said, Rod, about the United States becoming involved with the Mexican Government in a war against the French, and about Hank and me and the rifles. It is humbling to think that we, in a way however small, are a part of something so enormous. France? Mexico? Even the United States. They were only words to me until now. I don't know how to express it really, but, somehow, it makes me feel that there is a purpose beyond all things ordinary."

Rodrigo smiled warmly. "There is, Blake, my friend. There is a purpose for all things. You may never know specifically what it is, it will never be set to paper for you, but there is a purpose that will guide you to your destiny. You will never fully understand it, but you will be a servant to it."

Rodrigo placed his hands on the table and pushed the chair back with his legs. "Now, the sun is set. Enough philosophical speculation for one day. Let us meet with Benito. You won't be able to stay long, as there is much of importance for us to discuss. But it will be good for you to merely touch the hand of one so great. You will never forget that feeling."

The lingering rays of the dying sun flowed like death-blood through the square when they stepped from the *cantina*. Rodrigo set a brisk pace and they walked for nearly ten minutes before arriving at an unassuming hacienda situated on the edge of town. Two guards stood sentry beside the wide, arched doorway which was open with the exception of a latticework of strung beads suspended from the top of the door jamb. Rodrigo nodded to the guards and greeted them cordially before parting the beads and stepping inside, sweeping the sombrero from his head as he did so.

The room was expansive, cool, and clean nearly to the point of excessiveness. Braided rugs of reds and browns muted the sparkling crispness of the highly polished hardwood floors, and handcrafted serapes and capes adorned the walls. The furnishings were tastefully chosen and obviously selected for convenience with no thought given to ostentatiousness. There was an almost holy atmosphere about the room, as though some divinity had chosen it as a place of earthly residence. A middle-aged, slightly plump lady entered the room soundlessly on slippered feet. She stopped before Rodrigo and there was no need to smile, her face was the mask of joviality.

"Good evening, Señor Rodrigo. I am pleased to see you again."

Rodrigo bowed from the waist. "The pleasure is mine, Señora Juárez. May I present an American friend? Blake Evans, this is Señora Juárez, the wife of our great leader, Benito."

Blake attempted to bow, but it was clumsy and stiff. Señora Juárez laughed softly and offered her hand daintily. "You are a guest and we will follow your American custom. I'm pleased to welcome you into our home."

"Thanks, ma'am," Blake managed as he gently gripped the extended fingers before they withdrew.

"Benito is in his study working on some papers. Please excuse me and I will bring him to you. Make yourselves comfortable, if you will."

She glided from the room with courtly grace and was gone. Blake watched her skirts vanish beyond the near wall and he looked at Rodrigo. "She is some lady, isn't she, Rod?"

"She is that and more. The lion is no stronger than his mate, my friend, and between them they represent the best of Mexico's two finest bloodlines."

"Two?"

"Yes, two. The señora is Mexican. Benito is an Indian from the state of Oaxaca."

Stunned, Blake had not long to recover before a man of medium build, wearing black pants, a black coat and a high-collared white shirt encircled at the neck by a reddish cravat of sorts, entered the room. Blake studied the face of Benito Pablo Juárez as he moved toward them. Dark, straight hair, parted crisply on the left and neatly clipped, sat atop a wide, flat forehead. Heavy black brows hooded his widely spaced eyes. A bold, finely chiseled nose dominated his face and rested above full but economical lips which were now forming into a smile. But it was the eyes that held Blake. The confidence, the determination, the boldness that told of the man's inner soul without benefit or need of words. There was a hint of mystery, of power, of humor and humility in those dark, imposing eyes, and Blake knew immediately that he was standing before the most magnificent human being he had ever seen in his life.

Rodrigo stepped forward and extended his hand as they met in the center of the room. Juárez spoke as their hands touched.

"My good friend, Rodrigo. Sorry to have kept you waiting. Juanita scolded me properly for my rudeness."

"Not at all, Benito, not at all," Rodrigo offered as each clasped the hand of the other. "I won't keep you long from your other important affairs. But first, let me introduce my friend. He is an American from the Oklahoma Territory. Benito Juárez, may I present Blake Evans."

Juárez stepped quickly toward Blake and accepted his handshake. "Pleased to meet you, Mr. Evans. Most pleased, indeed. And please accept my thanks from the Mexican people to yours. Your country is helping us in our moment of greatest need. Perhaps, one day, we will be able to repay the favor."

Blake was dumbfounded. Here he stood before the rightful President of Mexico and accepting thanks for the entire American nation. He struggled for the proper words.

"Thank you, sir. I am pleased to meet you. I guess we're helping all we can, but I don't know for sure."

Juárez nodded and held Blake's hand a moment longer. "Yours is a generous nation, Mr. Evans. They will help to the extent of their ability to give."

The hands dropped and Juárez turned toward Rodrigo. "May I offer you gentlemen a drink?"

Rodrigo looked at Blake, and Blake shook his head. For some reason, a desperate urge had come over him, driving him from the great power of the two men in the room and toward the *cantina* where he would find Hank and Biggie Munn. He wanted to hear laughter, to drink and know the pleasure of a woman's company. Anything to get away from the awesome responsibility of protecting and planning the future for a nation of people who were asleep in their beds at that hour and dreaming of an end to French rule.

"Thank you, Mr. Juárez. Thank you very much," Blake said. "But I think I'd better be going. Thank you for having taken the time to meet me and please give my regards to Mrs. Juárez. I really better be going. See you later, Rod."

With those words he was gone, fleeing down the street toward the beckoning lights of the *cantina*. After several minutes his pace slowed, but his hand continued to tingle and the words of thanks to a nation he did not know continued to ring in his ears.

## Chapter Eight

The soft light of dawn touched the lace curtains and Blake rose up on one elbow to gaze at the morning. The girl was gone, but he remembered her smooth skin, the delicate fragrance of her hair and the night of singing and dancing in the *cantina*.

A squadron of six soldiers were entering the square on the cobbled street below and he watched them, listening to the clatter of hooves on spirited horses prancing in the friskiness of a new day. The leader was a large, broad-shouldered man and Blake thought him vaguely familiar. A rider behind rattled off some rapid-fire words in Spanish, and Blake watched the big man throw back his head and laugh. The laughter drifted to the open window. It was a rough, coarse laugh of the type that originates deep within the stomach and escapes the mouth as a rumble. Blake froze as though the sound had struck him to stone.

That laugh? He knew he had heard it before, or one similar to it. Those soldiers? Six of them, mounted and led by a huge man. He had seen them before, but where? He leaned to the window and looked down; the squadron had passed by and was now receding down the street. They wore the mixed dress of Juárez's revolutionary army with sloping sombreros drooping across their shoulders. It can't have been them. But who? The tumblers whirled and clicked in his brain like the combination lock opening the doors of a giant vault. And then it came to him, and he was stunned. The shock and disbelief held him motionless for nearly a minute. Then, when he moved it was with urgency as though death counted the seconds wasted. He scrambled into his clothes, slammed his feet into his boots, grabbed his gun belt in one hand and hat in the other and raced down the hall to pound on Hank's door. No response, only gentle snoring. Blake pounded again even more furiously.

"Hank! Wake up, Hank! I've gotta talk to you!"

He heard the creaking of a bed followed by a grumble. "What the hell? Is that you, Blake?"

"Yes. Let me in."

"Go away. I'll see you in the morning."

"It is morning, damnit! Open the door!"

"Blake, for Christ's sake," the springs creaked more loudly and the frame groaned under the weight of a man rising, "we finally get to civilization where they've got a bed with real sheets and I'm trying to sleep in for once in my life," he could hear the pad of bare feet shuffling across the floor, "and here you are, at dawn for God's sake, pounding on the door like . . ."

The door opened and Blake sprang inside. "We gotta go back."

"To bed?" Hank said hopefully.

"No."

Hank yawned and scrubbed the sleep from his eyes. "Too bad, I think it's a helluva idea. Then where do we have to go back to?"

"To Fort Hastings."

Hank was awake with a jerk. "Go where?"

"Back to Fort Hastings."

"That worm must of got to your brain, son. Those folks back there don't like us, remember?"

"I don't care about that. We gotta go back, no ifs, ands or buts about it."

"Well, maybe you don't, but I've got a helluva lot of ifs, ands or buts. Like *if* we go back, they'll hang us for sure, *and* I ain't goin' back for nothin' or nobody, *but* if you're stupid enough to put your neck in the noose again, then jump to it. I ain't superstitious, but I ain't dumb either. The thought of a third last meal doesn't help my appetite one damned bit."

They stared at each other while Blake buckled on his gun belt then handed Hank's to him.

"Mind if I put my pants on first?" Hank asked wryly, pushing the gun away.

"Then get 'em on. But we are going back."

Hank looked up wearily from the hands pressed to his face and massaging a throbbing head. "Okay. Okay, I'll ask, since it seems to be the only sensible thing to do at this point. Why, Blake? Why do we have to go back?"

"Because I saw Big Luke Wyler."

"You what!? Go on back to bed, you're just having a bad dream. And so am I, which, I'll point out, wasn't the case five minutes ago."

"It wasn't a dream. I saw him."

"Where, damnit! Here? In Cananea?"

"No. But it was here in Cananea that I knew I saw him at the fort. I heard a Mexican laughing, and I knew."

Hank sank onto the bed and his face dropped to his hands. "Oh, God. Of all the people I could have tied up with, I've gotta get stuck with the biggest ringtail of the lot. He hears a guy laugh in Mexico and that tells him he saw somebody in Arizona." He looked up with head shaking. "You'll have to run that by me one more time, Blake. It was a long night last night, I think I drank a half an ounce more than I should have. I'm hung over, tired and ninety degrees away from the position I'd like to be in."

Blake pulled up a chair, and sitting down, leaned forward in his excitement and was a little too close to Hank's face for his liking. Hank shifted uncomfortably to one side while words tumbled from Blake's mouth.

"When Rod and me were leaving the fort, a detachment of cavalry passed close to us. I only glanced at them for a few seconds, but I thought I recognized the sergeant in the lead, vaguely anyway. I didn't think anything more about it, but it stuck in my mind. He was wearing a handlebar moustache, which I didn't remember, but I knew I'd seen him someplace before."

"Okay, I've got that. You think you saw somebody. Let's get on with it."

"This morning I was looking out the window, enjoying the dawn, and . . ."

"Oh, God."

". . . I saw a squadron of Juárez's troops, six men just like back at the fort. The guy in front was huge, just like Big Luke, as everybody called him at home . . ."

"The name might indicate that."

". . . and somebody said something and he laughed. That's when I knew I'd seen Luke Wyler."

Hank stood up and pulled on his pants. "Blake, I'm not the smartest guy in the world, I'll admit to that, but I am smart enough to know you aren't making a hell of a lot of sense. So you heard a guy laugh. What do you want us to do? Go back to Fort Hastings and ask the colonel if we can tell one of his big sergeants a joke? Come on, Blake!"

"I know it was him. That laugh was just like Wyler's. The Mexican didn't have a moustache, and when he threw his head back and laughed, I saw Luke Wyler's face. And he was wearing a cavalry uniform and leading a detachment of men outside Fort Hastings."

"What would Wyler be doing in the army?" Hank asked, jamming his feet irritatedly into his boots. "From what you told me, if they're so damned anxious to find somebody to hang, he'd be just the ticket."

"I don't know what he's doing in the army, but I know he is and I'll bet his brothers are with him. Tell me this, when Stearns arrested you, did the sergeant with him have a big handlebar moustache?"

Hank thought back. "Yeah. Yeah, I believe he did. Matter-of-fact, I know for sure he did."

"Did he have a gap between his front teeth?"

"Now that I think about it, yes, he did."

"Did you ever hear him laugh?"

"Yeah. Right after he kicked me in the butt."

"What'd it sound like?"

"Like the rumble of thunder before a storm. Only worse."

"Congratulations. You were kicked in the butt by Big Luke Wyler."

Hank studied his thoughts while he buttoned up his shirt, then he massaged his right buttock, remembering. He buckled on his gun belt and reached for his hat. "You know, Blake, I think we'd better go back there." He was reaching for the door now. "I think Wyler had a hand in tryin' to get my neck stretched. That don't set well with me. And, I'm not too fond of butt kickin's either."

Rodrigo and Biggie Munn were eating breakfast on the veranda of the hotel when Hank and Blake walked through the lobby. Munn waved a hamlike fist and Rodrigo touched a napkin to his lips.

"Morning, Hank, Blake. Rest well?"

"Tried to," Hank returned, pulling out a chair and sitting down, "but the Pinkerton man here got me up right after he woke the roosters."

Blake laughed and took a seat. "That guy'd sleep through a tornado, Rod. Mornin', Big."

The gypsy nodded while lowering his face to his plate.

"Breakfast?" Rodrigo asked. "Tortillas, steak and refried beans."

"That sounds good," Hank said as the waiter approached. "But first I think I'll sprinkle a little moisture on the fires of hell." He turned and spoke in Spanish to the waiter. "Two beers for my friend and myself. Then we'll have the same thing these gentlemen are having."

The waiter nodded with a gold-toothed smile and moved away, and Hank turned to Rodrigo. "The Pinkerton man's come with something that might interest you, Rod. Blake?"

Blake leaned forward slightly. "Hank and I are going back to Fort Hastings, Rod."

"Really? Why?"

"Partially because of what we talked about last night. And having met Mr. Juárez, I'd like to try and get those rifles back for him. Maybe I can do something, you know, from my country to his. And, the second reason is, I saw Big Luke Wyler. You remember, the guy my brother fell in with?"

"That's very interesting," Rodrigo allowed, his eyebrows arching in curiosity. "Where did you see this Big Luke Wyler?"

"He's in the army at Fort Hastings. I don't know why, but I can't believe it's legitimate."

"As I said, very interesting. When are you going back?"

"As soon as we finish breakfast."

Rodrigo rolled a cigarette and spoke as he shook the match out. "Then why don't we ride together? As you can see, Munn and I have already eaten."

Blake and Hank stared at the two men in stunned silence before Blake found his tongue.

"You're going back there too?"

"Yes. We need those rifles very badly. They could mean the difference in the war, and we haven't got time to wait for another shipment. We are planning a major offensive against Chihuahua, with a minor diversionary thrust against Ciudad Camargo. Chihuahua is the northernmost outpost of the Maximilian forces. It must be taken, but we will need modern weapons. In two weeks we will move against Ciudad Camargo. One week later, we will take Chihuahua. Benito is depending on Munn and myself, with six hand-picked men, he can spare no more, to return with those rifles in time for the attack on Chihuahua."

The food arrived and Blake picked at his plate, but he was no longer hungry. "I think we all have something in this," he said, pushing his plate aside and taking up the beer bottle. "Your rifles were stolen, Hank was framed, and I've got a personal debt to settle with Luke Wyler. What say we settle all our debts at the same time, the four of us?"

All heads at the table nodded, and Hank shoved in a forkful of beans and gestured toward Blake's plate. "Better eat, Blake. I think we've got our work cut out for us."

"I'm not hungry. All I want now is Wyler."

Rodrigo watched them and understood their relationship—the same as his with Munn. Two friends adrift on the sea of life. "And you, Hank?" he asked, raising a coffee cup to his lips.

Hank shoved in the last bit of tortilla and reached for his beer bottle. "I want Stearns."

Rodrigo smiled. "I suspected as much. But I must tell you, his name is not Captain Mathew Stearns."

"What?"

"No, it is not. I don't know what his given name is, but I know for a fact that it isn't Stearns."

"When did you find that out?" Blake asked.

"From the moment I first met him in Colonel Bibby's office."

Hank's fingers worked over a cigarette and tobacco tumbled onto the tabletop. "You mean you talked to him all that time and knew he was a phony all along?"

"Precisely."

"How do you know he isn't Stearns, Rod?" Blake asked.

"I was certain of it when my eyes first touched his face. But, just to be sure, I asked him a question. Do you remember when we let him go and I asked him if he had ever been to Mexico? Nogales, perhaps?"

Hank and Blake nodded.

Rodrigo dusted the ash from his cigarette into the tray. "I met the real Captain Mathew Stearns in Nogales. It was there that we negotiated the purchase of the weapons. He was the aide of General Strickland, a supporter of our cause. Captain Stearns was fair-haired with a blond moustache, as is the impostor, and he was a real gentleman. Our friend back at Fort Hastings cannot be accused of that."

Hank let out a wheezing breath. "Good God. What the hell's going on back there?"

"Yeah, what the hell is going on?" Blake asked, mostly to himself. "First Luke Wyler shows up and now Stearns turns out to be a phony. Who do you think he really is, Rod?"

Rodrigo pushed away from the table and stood. "I have no idea, gentlemen. Shall we go and find out?"

## Chapter Nine

Captain Stearns paced before the desk like a wild animal on a short leash. Spinning suddenly, he slammed his hands down hard enough to cause the monogrammed penholder to jump.

"Why?"

Colonel Bibby jerked back, ran a finger beneath his stiff collar and tried to control his fright. "Because the War Department says so, Captain." He cautiously raised the wrinkled telegram lying on his desk for Stearns to see.

Stearns waved it away impatiently then planted his hand again. "I've read that goddamned thing! But, I still want to know why. This is supposed to be my command!"

Nervously clearing his throat as he rose, Bibby assumed his military stance, knuckles against spine, and carefully moved a short distance away.

"No one could be more distressed about these developments than I am, Captain. Please be assured of that. I repeat, no one. Not even you. I felt it my responsibility, as senior officer, to report the loss of those weapons, the escape of the prisoners, the actions of that Mexican heathen and all the other tomfoolery that's been going on around here." He made a helpless gesture toward the telegram. "And that's the thanks I get," he moaned, then read from the telegram as though he were reading his own epitaph. "'You are to remain in command until the stolen weapons are recovered, the escapees returned and proper relations restored with the Mexican government represented by one Benito Pablo Juárez.'" Moving toward the whiskey bottle, he looked over his shoulder as he spoke. "Can we accomplish all that this afternoon, Captain? In a lifetime? In ten millennia?"

Stearns slammed the desk again before stalking to the window. The parade ground was vacant and soldiers lounged in the shade, leaning against buildings and walls. The captain's face became even more brittle and the blood pounded through his temples.

"This is not a fort, not an army installation! It's a retirement camp! I came here to command! And command I will. I'll bring this slopyard to the highest standards of military efficiency. I'll protect those silver shipments, the citizenry, bring the Indians to heel and exterminate those Mexican infiltrators! But, I can't spend the rest of my life searching for rifles I can't find, chasing two trail bums that I can't catch, and playing up to some Mexican rabble that probably stole both the rifles and the prisoners in the same week!"

Bibby raised his glass and peered cautiously over the rim at the enraged captain. He sighed heavily before mustering the courage for spoken words. "I have absolute faith in you, Captain. While I regret leaving here, I am anxious to take on new challenges. You're anxious to command. That telegram stands between your dream and mine. Until it is met to the letter, we have no alternatives. Care for a drink?"

"No, damn you! And your goddamned telegram to the War Department as well. That was stupid of you, Colonel. Very stupid." He was gone with a slam of the door which nearly pulled the hinges from the wall.

Bibby shook his head while he freshened his glass. "Such a temper! What has the service come to, I wonder?" He drank deeply and wondered.

Captain Stearns had walked halfway across the parade ground before remembering the soldiers lounging in the shade. Without breaking stride, he executed an abrupt right face and closed in on the soldiers, some of whom were now struggling to their feet while others continued to watch the captain's approach without concern. Stearns stopped before them and his face was livid with rage.

"Teeeeennnnnnnnsssssshutttt!"

The troopers standing snapped to attention while the others pretended to scramble to a standing position while slowly pulling themselves into a position of semi-erectness. Stearns eyed them coldly as he proceeded through the ranks, looking each soldier up and down as though examining a side of beef hanging and prepared for the butcher's knife.

"You men are a disgrace to the uniform, any uniform," he growled, continuing to prowl. "In one week from today, this outfit is going to be the sharpest in the entire United States Cavalry. And, we are going to begin now! There will be a full-dress inspection of your barracks promptly at five-thirty this afternoon. All passes are canceled. At fifteen minutes after reveille tomorrow morning there will be an equipment inspection of mounts and hardware. Weapons qualification at zero nine hundred hours. Any man who fails to score satisfactorily will be assigned to stable duty for a week. Are there any questions?"

Silence in the ranks.

"Sergeant Elliot!"

The big sergeant with the handlebar moustache moved one step forward. "Yaassir?"

"Dismiss the troops then come directly to my quarters."

"Yaaasir."

Stearns moved away briskly, erect and staring straight ahead. Sergeant Elliot turned toward the company without military precision. His brows lowered and a gleam came into his milky eyes.

"You fellers ain't been good little boys, an' the cap'n doan like that. Nor does I." He towered over the troops, many of whom were not yet out of the teens, glowering while the moustache curled into a sneering arch of triumph. "Now you're gonna do what the cap'n said, or I'll break your face personal-like and with pleasure. You hear me good, boys?"

The troops mumbled and shifted nervously. Sergeant Elliot nodded his approval. "Corporal Thatcher, Corporal Culhane, Private Moody and Private Davidson! Prepare your mounts and be front and center in one half hour. I gotta hunch we got some patrollin' to do after I talk with the captain. The resta you ratbags is dismissed."

The troops broke formation and moved toward the barracks in groups of twos and threes. One young soldier, after glancing over his shoulder to make sure Elliot was out of earshot, spoke in low tones to his companions.

"That's the way it always is. Him and those bastards from that lost detachment get all the good duty. The only thing the rest of us get is the shaft."

Another man nodded. "That's a mighty queer outfit, ever danged one of 'em except Corporal Thatcher. Darnedest thing, I asked Corporal Culhane if he'd fought at Gettysburg? Know what? He said he'd never heard of it."

The third trooper agreed. "Davidson ain't no better. Other day, we was walkin' across the parade ground together? The mole, Colonel Bibby, was out of his quarters for some reason and we met him? Know what?"

"He didn't salute," offered one.

"Yep he did, right enough. But with his left hand."

They laughed, shaking their heads as they approached the barracks steps. The first speaker bounded up, then stopped on the top step. "They lost fourteen men in the skirmish, right? Well, if that fourteen was anything like what survived, I think we got us some bandidos to thank."

They were inside the barracks now and two of them sat down on their bunks facing each other while the third placed his boot heavily on the rail and leaned down. "Corporal Thatcher ain't exactly easy to understand neither. I fought in the first battle of Bull Run—lost a cousin and a brother. Me and Thatcher was talkin' the other day. Well, more like I was talkin' and he was listenin'; don't talk much, that feller. Anyway, I was tellin' about the battle, and he got right up in the middle and said it wasn't Bull Run, it was Manassas. Kinda like he was challengin' me, you know? Well, I didn't say nothin' and walked away. He's as hot-tempered as they come, and sort of cold, like a snake, and I didn't want no part of him."

"Manassas? That's what the Rebs called the battle."

"I'm knowin' that. What the hell is a corporal in the United States Cavalry doin' usin' Reb names?"

Corporal Thatcher came through the doorway and the men fell silent, busying their hands and wondering about the steely-eyed corporal.

The river was a snake, twisting its casual way through the brilliant moonlight. Frogs ceased to croak when the horses neared and their singular plops into the water were accented by the stillness. The verdant green of tall water grass contrasted sharply with the breasting wasteland and crickets maintained a constant squeaking hum, dying as the riders approached then picking up again as they passed by.

Hank twisted in the saddle and studied a solitary butte. "This is about where I crossed, Rod," he said, checking the stars again. "Should be close, anyway."

They pulled up and listened to the quiet with the gentle sound of horses munching grass over the soft jangle of bit chains adding to the night symphony. Rodrigo's eyes studied the mild slope of the river bank. "You say Stearns said they followed the wagon to approximately this point, lost the trail, then picked up your tracks, Hank?"

"That's what he said, but he ain't told the truth till yet, so I don't put a helluva lot of faith in it."

"He may have been. At least we have to go on that assumption. That means the ambush occurred some distance upstream, they lost the trail between here and there, and if the wagon actually did enter the water, there should still be some imprints where the ground is moist but not muddy. How deep was the river when you crossed?"

"Breastbone high to a horse, no more."

"That wagon was loaded with rifles. It wouldn't float, so whoever took them, if they crossed the river, now has three hundred Spencers rusting in their cases." He paused and stared into the dark water. "If they crossed the river, that is."

"They'd have to cross, wouldn't they, Rod?" Blake asked. "That ambush happened on the south side of the river. Unless they took those rifles to Mexico, they'd have to cross somewhere."

"Yes. But where, if they did cross?"

Hank scratched his head, tilting his hat over his eyes before pushing it back. "Ain't we about a day late and a dollar short on this, Rod? Surely the army sent a patrol back here and tried to pick up a trail after Stearns and me and the rest of 'em got to the fort."

"You might be correct in that assumption, Hank, but I think not. Stearns, or whatever his name is, obviously has Colonel Bibby convinced both of his identity and integrity. If he was involved in the theft, those troops would never have been sent anywhere near where the rifles might be hidden. Hank, you and Blake take three of my men and search east along the river. Munn and I and the others will work west. Meet before daylight in the draw at the bottom of the butte. It faces west, so we can keep the horses there and watch the river during daylight from the top of the butte."

The cold gray hush that precedes the coming dawn settled over the desert. Blake thought he should turn back to reach the butte before daylight, but he was nearing a grove of cottonwoods that touched the river then fanned out to the limit of moisture in the scorched earth. After hesitating, he decided to cross the stand of timber before quitting the search.

He ducked his head to clear a low hanging branch and the horse picked its way carefully through the dead limbs and downed trees. The stand was thick, and it felt to Blake as though he had ridden into night again. The grove was wider than he had realized, so, with one long last look at the river bank, he pulled the horse's head up and swung the animal around. He leaned low in the saddle to clear another branch, then the reins snapped tight in his hand. The horse pranced to one side and Blake stared down at something white against the greenness of the grass-covered, sandy soil.

Stepping from the saddle, Blake carefully plucked the palm-sized object from the grass. He ran a thumb over the rough fiber and stared into the dense foliage. Now what the hell's a woodchip doing here? he asked himself, glancing around for more but seeing none. Leading the horse now, with the chip in hand, he moved into the grove away from the stream. Another chip and then two more. And the ground was scarred from something heavy having been dragged.

Curiosity overwhelmed him. The white-gray, mottled tree trunks were becoming visible now, and he knew he should mount and ride. But he continued on, following the scars and increasing trail of woodchips. Then he saw the first stump. And as the dull light of dawn filtered into the grove, he saw more, perhaps twenty or thirty white, rough stumps protruding out of the ground like so many amputated legs. He stood among them, staring at the browning leaves, and he knew where the wagon had gone. Or, at least how it had gone wherever it had gone. He scooped a handful of chips into his hat, grabbed a handful more, then swung onto the saddle.

The first rays of sunlight touched the edge of the grove as the horse cantered from the foliage. Blake touched spurs to flanks and could see the probing fingers of dawn turning the crest of the butte a brilliant golden color while the night clung tenaciously to its lower reaches. Hank was galloping toward him and he could faintly make out three dust trails streaking toward the shadowed object in the distance.

"Where the hell'uve you been?" Hank shouted as they raced side by side toward their sanctuary. "Pickin' mushrooms?"

"No. Just pickin'," Blake returned, grinning with the hat clutched to his chest.

They pounded into the ravine and the instant heat of day was a glare on their faces. Blake jumped down, threw the reins to the Mexican standing guard over the horses and scrambled to the top of the butte. Clawing with both hands and ducking the pebbles torn free by Blake's churning boots, Hank also worked his way to the crest.

Rodrigo and Munn were lowered into a deep wind depression on the west side of the mountain top, and Rodrigo was already studying the ground below with a pair of field glasses. The fort was faintly visible on the horizon and the twin buttes near the town of the same name thrust out of the desert like humps on a camel's back.

Lowering himself into the hole, Blake pulled the hat from beneath his arm. "I found it, Rod," he panted.

Rodrigo lowered the glasses. "Found what, Blake?" he asked, looking first at the chips then at Blake.

"Where the wagon went. Or, I should say, how it went." He caught his breath. "Phewwww. That's some climb."

Rodrigo examined the chips carefully. "Are you thinking what I'm thinking?" he asked, looking up at Blake.

"Raft?"

"Raft."

"Then I'm thinkin' what you're thinkin'. The stumps are fresh cut, and it damned sure wasn't beavers."

"Where?"

"Upstream about three, maybe four miles."

Hank scrambled into the hole. "Lord God, son," he grunted leaning against the smooth rock, "that's some climb. Whatcha got in the hat?"

"Chips."

"Buffalo?"

"Human."

"Make a poor fire."

"How many stumps were there, Blake?" Rodrigo asked, fingering the white wood.

"Twenty at least. Maybe more."

Rodrigo's calculating eyes went to the winding ribbon below them. "So, that's how they did it," he mused out loud. "I wonder, I just wonder, if those rifles aren't down there somewhere right now, hidden and waiting for the right people to come for them."

They all looked down at the river with cottonwood groves dotting its twisted course at spaced intervals to the horizon.

Rodrigo's mind continued its probing search and he spoke in an inquiring voice. "How far would they take them, to be safe yet accessible? And, once we find them, how long will it be before someone comes to get them? If they haven't already."

"How are we going to find them, Rod?" inquired Blake. "They're sure as hell not just parked in one of those groves."

"No, I'm sure they're not. They can't be in water, can they? And they can't be in the open. There wasn't enough time between when Hank crossed the river and when he was captured for them to have been taken very far into the desert. But you said"—Rodrigo turned slightly toward Hank—"they claimed they followed the wagon tracks out of the river and lost them in the rocky soil. He told the truth about following the trail to the river. I wonder if he's lying now?"

"Stearns would climb a tree just to tell a lie when standing on the ground would do him more good."

"The criminal mind is interesting, Hank," Rodrigo said, offering a weak smile. "I believe they are hidden along the river somewhere."

Hank shook his head. "Naw, couldn't be. I say they went inland with them. Deserted mine somewhere, or sold them already."

"To whom?"

"Beats me. Indians maybe?"

"Indians wouldn't have that kind of money."

"Okay. But they're not along the river."

"Bet?"

"What?"

"Tequila?"

"Quart?"

"Agreed."

"You're on."

A buzzard hung motionless in the stilled sky, its wings hooded and a patch of blue showing through the black where several feathers were missing. It might have been sleeping, or intent on its prey, so calmly it rested on its unnested perch far above the ground. Once the faintest beat of its wings, then loss of animation again. Rodrigo's eyes had gone to the bird and he watched it. Suddenly and without forewarning, the wings dipped and the buzzard spiraled down in concentric sweeps. Rodrigo nodded.

"The Indians call them the sentinels of the desert. Nothing escapes their eyes, nothing lives without their knowledge, and nothing dies without their visitation. Constantly they watch, patient like the desert which sustains them. They know no urgency short of surprise, they take no more than they need and need nothing more than they take. They wait for death and death comes to them faithfully."

The dark Argentinian looked at Hank, Blake and Munn, each in turn. "We will be the desert sentinels. From this butte we will watch and wait. Those who kill will come to us, and like the true sentinels of the desert, we will descend upon them and take what is rightfully ours. For you, Blake? Vengeance. For Hank? Revenge. For Munn and myself? The instruments of freedom for all the oppressed of Mexico."

Rodrigo stared at the three men for long moments as though consumed by his thoughts. Then he broke away and resumed his position with the glasses once again. "Tonight we search the river. For now, Blake, you and Hank sleep in the shade of the arroyo. In four hours you will relieve Munn and me. We will continue the procedure until we have fallen on our prey."

Sergeant Elliot rapped once on the door then stepped into the captain's cabin. The shutters were closed and the room was cool in the semi-darkness. "You wanted to see me, Cap'n?"

"Yes. I thought we could rely on Bibby's ignorance, but now he has used that stupidity against us. He is reassigned here until the weapons are found, the prisoners captured and the exchange made with Juárez. We are going to have to adjust our plans accordingly."

"Like what? Arrange an accident for the good colonel?"

"No. After what's happened, an accident of any type would bring an Inspector General down on us immediately."

Elliot eyed the captain suspiciously. "You're not talkin' about giving the rifles back, are you? That's fifteen thousand dollars! I've had about all the army I can stand, and I ain't givin' up that kinda change."

Stearns crossed to peek out the window, then, satisfied, he leaned against the night stand. "Control your voice. We aren't giving anything away. We'll get our money, the army will get its rifles back and Bibby will be on his way."

Sergeant Elliot crossed the room and snatched a whiskey bottle from the shelf and poured angrily. "I've let you call all the shots on this thing, friend, and that ain't my normal way." He turned and his moustache drooped around the glass in a curling sneer. "And if you, Jason T. Burke, think I'm gonna let those rifles go for nothin', what with Dubois headin' this way right now with fifteen thousand, you'd better take another long hard think. Big Luke is in this for all the marbles, and like I said, he's gettin' just a little sick a playin' soldier boy."

Burke's eyes hardened and his military posture stiffened automatically. "I am Captain Mathew Stearns, and until this thing is over, you are Sergeant Tom Elliot." His voice was a low, threatening hiss. "No other names will be used, not even in private. Is that understood, *Sergeant* Elliot?"

Big Luke watched the smaller man over his glass. There was a coiled deadliness about him, the posture of a mountain lion set to spring. And, there was a vicious cunning in his eyes as though he considered size to be no factor in a fight. Big Luke remembered the passionless executions of sixteen men and how the chill had traced his spine as Burke had stood, pistol in hand, over the head of Captain Mathew Stearns. The chill touched his spine again now, and he drank deeply to control the shudder. He lowered the glass carefully and wiped a sleeve across his mouth, attempting to be casual.

"Okay, Cap'n, have it your way. How do we get our money for the rifles and still hand 'em over to the army?"

Burke knew the threat had passed and that he had won. He

smiled easily and poured a ration of whiskey for himself and another for the sergeant.

"In the same way we obtained them originally. Take your patrol to the river now. Make sure that nothing has happened, no one has been near them. Don't go to them yourself, just close enough to be certain. That's enough for right now, I'll explain the rest of it to you when you and I and your unit go on another patrol tonight." The captain turned the glass in his hand and stared into the liquid. "You see, Sergeant Elliot, you are going to find something this afternoon that hadn't been there before. Tracks that had not been seen before. Bibby's desperate, and he'll go along with anything I say as long as he gets those rifles back. Before we meet with Dubois, everything will have been arranged."

The sergeant laughed with lusty cruelty and downed the whiskey in a single gulp. He mopped his moustache again as he stomped toward the door. "I think I know what you've got in mind, Cap'n. And I love it. Me an' the boys'll just mosey on down there right now and find those tracks."

The blazing sun arched a scorching path through the middle of the universe and the desert shimmered with reverberating waves of heat slamming against the white sand and shuddering with the impact. The butte was hatless to the sun and the cool of slanting shadows was lost to the piercing blaze above.

Blake was lying in the depression, a blanket hot beneath his chest and eyes pressed to the binoculars as they swept the desert in a constant, probing search. Hank lay to the rear under a piece of canvas stretched over the depression and held in place with rocks atop the four corners. An hour had passed and Blake would soon trade with Hank for the final hour of their shift. When Rodrigo and Munn arrived, they would quit the butte to sleep in the relative coolness of the arroyo.

Blake started to pull the glasses away to brush the trickles of sweat from the corners of his eyes, but the glasses snapped back at the last instant. The hot metal of the binoculars pressed against his tortured skin and he searched out the tiny specks below. "Here they come," he muttered, working the focus adjustment.

"Huh? Huh, what?" Hank asked, stirring beneath the primitive shelter.

They were in full view now, riding at an easy gallop and Blake counted six of them with the blue of their uniforms brilliant against the sea of white. He focused on the huge rider in the lead, and, even though he could not recognize him from that distance, he knew the man. His pulse beat quickened and the hard metal ground against his face. And the black hatred touched the corners of his mind.

Hank's boots scraped on barren rock as he clawed his way forward. "Whatcha got?"

Blake's eyes never left the glasses. "They're coming, Hank. Get Rod."

Instinctively, Hank started to peer over the ledge but ducked back down. "Who's comin'?"

"Wyler. Get Rod."

Hank crawled away and Blake watched the detachment slow by the river's edge and stop for the horses to drink. He thought he could almost hear voices in the clear air. The horses moved into the stream, fording the river just below where the wagon had gone in and Rodrigo's fingers touched Blake's shoulder.

"How many?"

"Six. Luke Wyler and five troopers. Here, see what you think," Blake said, hunching down and sliding away as he handed the glasses across.

Rodrigo pulled his hat off, adjusted the span of the binoculars for his narrow face and cautiously rose to the lip of the butte. The horses were struggling up the opposite bank now and turning west. They were lost to Rodrigo's view as they passed through a stand of cottonwoods, but he picked them up again on the other side. They rode down river for several hundred yards before pulling up at a place where the river made a sweeping curve to the right. They were just on the edge of another grove and Rodrigo cursed, knowing that if they entered the trees they would be lost to his sight.

But the big rider urged his horse down the bank and into the river. The horse swam, drifting with the current, then rose majestically in the center of the channel with a sandbar beneath its hooves. Rodrigo watched, fascinated, and he knew the rider had been there before. The horse was in the middle of the curve now. Its rider urged it into the channel on the far side of the sandbar, and the current carried horse and rider to a stretch of beach in the deepest portion of the river's bend. The big man moved toward a depression in the river bluff, dark to Rodrigo's eyes, before stopping with the horse standing just at the river's edge. After nearly a minute of studying the dark object, he turned the horse and re-entered the water. The current swept them around the bend and out of sight.

The glasses went back to the five riders waiting beside the grove and, after five minutes, a horse emerged from the shadows and the big man rode into the sunlight. He motioned to the others and they turned west again and the stand of cottonwoods plucked them from the blistering glare of the desert.

Rodrigo lowered the glasses and slid down with his back to the scorched rock. "I think we have found the location of our rifles," he said vaguely, his mind still sorting facts from conjecture.

"Where?" Blake asked.

"There's a big, sweeping bend in the river about a mile downstream from the crossing. There appears to be a cave there. And, I think that cave contains one wagon and three hundred rifles."

"How can you be sure?"

"I'm not. But Wyler went to that spot and I *am* sure he's been there before. His horse drifted with the current to a wide, sandy beach, just like a raft would have done."

Puzzled, Blake shook his head. "Why would he go to the rifles in broad daylight?"

"Because he is sure of himself. Overconfidence is our best—

and only—ally, Blake. They think we are in Mexico, and Bibby is no threat to them." Rodrigo's eyes went to the stark blue sky. "I wonder if he was just checking on them, or preparing to make an exchange."

"Did they leave?"

"Yes, toward the west."

"I didn't see anyone else. Who would they be dealing with?"

"If my assumptions are correct, we'll find that out tonight. But, put yourself in their position. There's a war going on one hundred miles to the south. You've stolen the weapons from one side, weapons that side desperately needs, and you want to get the highest price for them. To whom would you go for that price?"

Blake shrugged. "To the other side, I guess. To Maximilian?"

Rodrigo nodded and pulled his hat on again. "It's merely speculation on my part, but if I were them, that's exactly what I would do. And I believe that is what they are preparing to do. You go below now, send Munn up and get some sleep. Tonight, hopefully, the desert sentinels will leave their perch and fall upon their prey."

Blake started to go, then hesitated. "You know, Rod, a strange sensation passed through me when I saw Wyler through the glasses. It was the same thing I felt when I knew I would kill my brother."

"I can understand that. He is in death's debt. Perhaps you will be the one to collect."

"I hadn't really thought much about him, or his brothers. But now, after having seen him, the black hatred is there again. The same black hatred I had to force upon my mind when I went after Will. Now it's coming naturally and, I'll admit, it scares me."

Reaching for the makings, Rodrigo rolled a cigarette and watched Blake's face as his fingers worked tobacco into paper. "Killing for no purpose, for the wrong purposes, is the worst thing a man can do. But, sometimes, killing for a certain purpose is the right and only thing for a man to do. A man lives by his instincts, and they will lead him to his destiny. Your black hatred, as you call it, is your basic instinct born of the loss of your family. The Wylers are an extension of that loss. Your instinct is to kill them, and unless they are more crafty than you, you probably will." Rodrigo drew deeply on the cigarette and exhaled smoke into a cupped hand. "When the time comes, let no hesitation cross your mind. If it does, you will be dead."

Blake nodded. "I'll remember, and thanks. You seem to understand this business of death and killing a bit better than I."

The Argentinian smiled wanly. "No one understands it, Blake, my friend. Some are forced into it, as I was, and others come to it willingly. But no one understands it. One moment a man is alive, the next he is dead. And the victor has the remainder of his life to live with the consequences of his success. It will never leave you, Blake. Each man you kill has stolen a piece of your soul. But, you have no choice. It is kill or be killed, the constant drumbeat of the animal world. And the good die just as quickly as the bad." Rodrigo squashed the cigarette out and reached for the binoculars again. "Get some rest now, I think you will need it for the coming night. And tell your friend Hank that he owes me a quart of tequila."

Blake scurried, hunched over, to the trail leading down to the arroyo, making his way carefully to the bottom and turning to the welcome coolness. Then he froze, and his heart leaped into his throat.

Biggie Munn moved swiftly through the shadows with what appeared to be the lifeless form of a man draped over his shoulder. Hank's head hung down and glazed eyes stared sightlessly, sunken in a chalk-white face.

## Chapter Ten

Munn gently lowered the sprawling, limp body against the wall, and the horses held there backed away with a nervous snort. The three Mexicans looked up from their card game with curious, concerned eyes and watched Munn strip the sock from Hank's bootless left foot. Swelling bloated the skin to nearly the bursting point and red lines traced twin streaks from his instep to his calf.

Rushing forward, Blake knelt beside Munn, who was now easing the big knife from its sheath.

"What happened, Munn? What happened to Hank? He isn't . . . dead . . . is he?"

Munn glanced across and Blake remembered that questions were useless. His blue eyes were clear and gave not the slightest hint of anxiety or concern. He shook his head then set to his work.

The knife point touched pale skin and blood burst forth in a spurt. He made two tiny crossed slashes, laid the knife on the ground, and drew Hank's foot to his mouth. After sucking hugely, he turned his head and spat, red spittle smacking the floor of the arroyo. Munn sucked again and Blake watched both in fear and fascination. Blood streaked from Munn's mouth a second, then a third time. Hank remained unconscious, and when Munn motioned toward the canteen, Blake scrambled to retrieve it. The gypsy rinsed his mouth carefully then washed the swollen skin now turning black on the sole of Hank's foot. Then he sat back, rolled a cigarette and grinned at Blake.

Blake stared at him in startled confusion. He gestured toward Hank with empty palms and shrugged. Munn just grinned. Remembering that, although Munn could not speak, he could hear, Blake watched him with discerning eyes.

"What happened, Biggie?"

Munn squiggled his fingers like a crab before stabbing a finger to indicate a sting.

"Scorpion?"

Munn nodded, again with a grin.

"How big?"

Munn shrugged, stood and left the shelter. Seconds later he was back with a black, ugly creature lying on the broad blade of his knife. He dropped the crushed animal by Blake's boots and laughed when Blake jumped back. Nearly four inches in length, the blackish-yellow animal appeared to be as lethal in death as it had in life. Blake turned it over with the toe of his boot and saw the hooked tail with its stinger missing.

Hank moaned and Blake sprang to his side, and taking the bandanna from his neck, he moistened it with water to dampen Hank's forehead and parched lips. Hank moaned again and nibbled at the trickle of water. Blake forced the lips apart and sprinkled more water into Hank's mouth. Hank lapped the moisture thirstily and his eyes opened. At first a crack, then wider.

"Scorpion," he said weakly before slumping back against the wall, unconscious again.

Blake cast a worried glance upward as Munn rose and nodded toward the butte, and when the gypsy was gone, he looked at the scorpion again with its tail arched as if to strike at death itself.

An hour passed before Rodrigo came into the arroyo, lifted each of Hank's eyelids and checked his pulse. Rolling a cigarette, he squatted and handed the makings across to Blake while scraping a match against the rock wall.

"I would have come sooner, Blake, but there was no need. The sting of the scorpion is much like the bite of a rattlesnake. If the poison is extracted quickly enough, there is little chance of death. If not, survival depends on the strength of the victim's heart. Hank is doing for himself the only thing that can be done; remain calm, keep the blood flow to a minimum and wait for the pain."

Rodrigo drew on the cigarette and squinted through the smoke. "When the pain comes, he will be conscious and out of danger."

"When the pain does come, how bad is it?"

Rodrigo shrugged. "Like that of a thousand wasps."

"God! How'd he get stung?"

"Munn and I can communicate through hand signals and lip reading as well as you can with a man wearing a whole tongue. He said Hank pulled his boots off and started to go to sleep after he came from the butte. He rested a moment then went to relieve himself. He neglected to put his boots on again. The scorpion, like all creatures of the desert, including the desert itself, is unforgiving of carelessness."

"Will he be able to ride tonight?"

"No. It will be at least a day before his foot becomes small enough to fit into a boot."

Blake eyed Rodrigo suspiciously. "We can't just leave him here."

"Yes we can. They will come for the rifles tonight."

"No, Rod, goddamnit! To hell with the rifles! Hank comes first!"

The dark eyes, displaying no emotion, held steady on Blake's face. "That is your decision to make. I have none. A land of a million people are being denied their right to their homeland, and they make my decisions for me. Hank is entirely capable of taking care of himself, and better off by far than trying to ride with us. Or ride anywhere, for that matter. I need your help, if you feel you can give it freely. If not, then you will be of no help to me or my cause. As I said, it is your decision to make."

"Goddamn a bunch of scorpions!" Blake raged. "What a helluva time to get stung!"

Rodrigo smiled easily. "There is no good time to get stung,

Blake. It's just that some times are worse than others. Let's prepare some food, then I will go up and relieve Munn."

Rodrigo moved toward the pack saddles stacked in the far end of the arroyo, and after a last careful glance at Hank, Blake hunched to his feet on creaking knees to follow.

Lithe fingers worked over leather thongs and Rodrigo called to the Mexicans and they came forward to remove tortillas, beans, chili and dried beef from earthenware containers. Using his tortilla as a plate, Rodrigo spread on a layer of beans, laced it with chili, selected a strip of beef, and rolled it into a compact cylinder.

Blake duplicated the procedure, covering the beans entirely with the delicious smelling, aromatic chili. Rodrigo watched, taking a bite and reaching for the wineskin. A fine trail of purple squirted into his up-tilted mouth and he chewed methodically as Blake hungrily tore off a bite. There was silence in the draw and all eyes watched Blake's face.

The flavor was incredibly delicious at first. Then the heat began. He could feel it swelling his neckline, beads of perspiration broke out on his forehead, and his eyes filled with boiling, hazy moisture.

Blake swallowed hard and the food passed, but the heat remained. He tried to talk and his eyes blinked in slow repetitions like he might have been a giant bullfrog sitting by a pond. The Mexicans had waited and Blake provided their reward. They howled uproariously, heaped on the chili in thrice the amount as had Blake, and leaned back to eat without the slightest trace of discomfort.

The wineskin passed around and finally it was in Blake's outstretched hand. He aimed the opening toward what was to him a flaming inferno and squeezed. Wine splashed across his cheeks, neck and chin, and by the time it found his mouth, the stream had died to a trickle. He squeezed again. Nose and chin this time, but a stream of moisture finally passed through his searching lips.

The Mexicans howled again and Blake grinned through the

wine dripping from his face. "Holy Christ, Rod," he wheezed. "What is that stuff anyway?"

"Chili. Good for you. Keeps the worms down."

"A fire-breathing dragon wouldn't have a chance against that stuff. That's hot!"

Rodrigo turned toward the grinning Mexicans. *"Que est muy kilo, Francisco?"*

The lean young Mexican stopped grinning long enough to take a huge bite. He chewed as though giving the question maximum concentration before flashing another expansive grin.

"No, Señor Rodrigo. *Es poquito frio.*"

The others laughed as Rodrigo turned to Blake again. "I asked him if it was hot, but he said, no, it is a little too cool. Scrape some off and eat, my friend. It is good for you. The Mexicans claim that the heat of the chili wards off the heat of the sun so they can work longer in the fields." He paused with a sly wink. "That doesn't explain their two-hour afternoon siesta, but what does it matter? They like to think it anyway."

After preparing four huge tortillas, Rodrigo draped a wineskin over his neck and turned toward the butte. "When Hank awakens, give him some wine from one of the other skins. Have him eat whatever he can keep down and lie still. I must return to Munn. He hasn't eaten, and he gets very mean when he's hungry."

Blake watched Rodrigo work his way through the outcroppings of rock like a mountain cat before scraping the chili from his tortilla and eating with relish. Forsaking the chili, he ate a second and a third before taking a long drink from the wineskin. Then he went and stretched out beside Hank and slept.

Long shadows were creeping up the far wall when Blake awoke with a start with the first moan escaping from Hank's mouth. Scrambling to his knees, he drew the wineskin up and pulled the plug. The wine dribbled onto Hank's lips and slid away. Blake persisted, forcing the pale lips apart and squeezing again with the other hand. Hank licked at the wine as though his tongue were frozen, and finally he swallowed a decent mouthful. His eyes batted several times before opening halfway.

"You're runnin' up quite a doctor bill, Hank. Gonna have to pay up pretty soon."

Hank swallowed and tried to grin. "Take it out in pain. Feels like somebody chopped off my left foot. It hurts like the devil stuck his fork in it, and the rest of those sinners down there in hell was jumpin' up and down on it."

"You did come close enough for him to take a stab at it, I reckon. But a big, black scorpion gets most of the credit. You should have more sense than to go wandering around in the desert without your boots on."

"Never been accused of havin' much sense. But, in this case, nature was callin' pretty loud and I was in a helluva hurry to reply. How bad's it look?" Hank asked, attempting to raise his foot up for a look and failing.

"Like you've got the gout in one leg. Rod says it'll take a day or two for the swelling to go down."

"How much wine we got?"

Blake glanced toward the pack saddles. "Quite a bit, I guess."

Hank closed his eyes, leaned back and opened his mouth again. "Just keep on pourin', son, just keep on pourin'. Ain't never had pain like this before."

Blake waited beside Hank until he dozed into a fitful sleep before placing the wineskin on his friend's stomach and moving toward the butte.

The sun was half-cupped in the hand of the wasteland horizon and color splashed across the faded desert like mountain flowers bursting forth in spring. Munn's shaved head glistened a deep brown in the dying rays, and his elbows were cocked on the ledge as he watched the land below through the binoculars.

"Anything moving yet, Rod?" Blake asked as he crawled toward the Argentinian.

"Nothing. How's Hank?"

"Drinking wine and complaining to beat hell. I think he's gonna be all right."

Rodrigo nodded. "He will be."

The first kiss of evening breeze touched the butte and carried a rush of heat from the desert floor. The wind increased in proportion to the sun's lowering position in the sky, and when twilight closed about the mountain perch strong winds curled and licked at their ageless adversary.

Rodrigo studied the wind in the closing darkness and Blake felt the brim of his hat dip and fold as though it were being moulded by soft, invisible hands.

"What time we goin', Rod?" Blake asked.

"We, Blake?"

Blake cupped his hands to light a cigarette. "Yeah, we. Hank would be disappointed if both of us missed the fun."

"I'm sure he would. When the moon is full up. I want to make sure that wagon is where I think it is before Wyler comes back."

"What kind of plan have you got in mind?"

"To play our hand, one card at a time."

Blake shivered and pulled the collar up about his neck. "Damn it gets cold in a hurry. Boiling one minute and freezing the next."

Rodrigo nodded, watching the brilliant white ball rise higher in the sky. "Yes, it does. The desert is much like a woman's heart. Passionate and hating, both in the same instant." Then he fell silent, and Blake could sense the distance between them. He knew this strange, fierce man beside him was planning, thinking, revising. And preparing to kill.

The other riders were mounted and waiting in the mouth of the arroyo while Blake stooped, holding the reins slack in his hand.

"You gonna be all right, Hank?"

Hank looked up from the ground with his left foot resting on a blanket, a Colt across his waist, the wineskin across his stomach and his rifle propped against the canyon wall.

"Hell yes, I'm gonna be all right. But I sure wish these fellers would learn to drink out of a bottle." He indicated the wineskin with a helpless motion. "I wind up wearing more than I drink from this damned little bag."

"I found that out the hard way myself. But you'll manage, I'm sure of that, Hank. When it comes to a man getting booze between his lips, you're holding high card all the way."

"Get the hell out of here, if you ain't got nothin' decent to say. And don't let that damned horse step on my foot!"

"Take care of yourself," Blake said, swinging into the saddle and joining the others now moving from the sanctuary.

They rode in a single-file column and their horses' hooves pounded the packed alkali soil with firm, muffled beats. The white flood of moonlight had stolen the color again from the desert and shadows stretched long and black as though the sun were shining. But the sun wasn't shining, and Blake was glad for the thick sheepskin jacket fitted snugly across his shoulders. His fingers worked the buttons on the coat as his horse galloped behind Francisco's.

They angled toward the nearest grove of cottonwoods and the wide band of silver that was the river. It was like stepping from daylight into darkness when the horses cantered beneath the spreading canopy and Rodrigo slowed the pace to watch for fallen logs and limbs.

Blake recognized the place where the wagon had gone into the river, and he knew they were no more than a mile from the sweeping curve. A chill crept up his spine and a cold shiver skipped across his shoulders, but his face felt hot and flush. He eased the Colt in his holster and instinctively reached behind to touch the cool wooden stock of his Winchester. It would be his first time in battle, and he wondered momentarily about courage. Then he cleared his mind and stared ahead through the filtered patches of moonlight.

They stayed clear of the river's edge to avoid leaving tracks for several hundred yards before Rodrigo finally pulled up. Blake urged his horse forward, along with the others, to form a semicircle around the Argentinian. The gurgle of water, now rushing toward the sweeping bend, murmured in the stillness. The large grove of cottonwoods stood silently before them like blackened ghosts, and Blake listened for a few seconds to the rattling croak of frogs and hum of singing crickets.

Rodrigo studied the bend for long moments before turning. He spoke rapidly but softly in Spanish, and Blake heard his name mentioned but understood nothing of what was being said. The other riders moved silently toward the cottonwoods, and Blake hesitated when Rodrigo turned to face him.

"Blake, the others will cover us from the trees. You and I will enter here, where Wyler did, cross to the sandbar and let the current take us to the dark spot. Hold your weapons above your head and be prepared. If the night creatures fall silent while we are at midstream, get to the trees as quickly as you can."

Nodding, Blake unbuckled his gun belt and pulled the Winchester from its scabbard. He nudged his horse toward the riverbank behind Rodrigo's, and the cold, oily water quickly went to his knees. He looked down and the water was black now, the silver had gone and the sickening tug of the current swept him away as he slid from the saddle on the upstream side.

When he felt the horse's flailing hooves touch solid ground, Blake eased into the saddle again and Rodrigo rose majestically out of the water before him. They moved along the sandbar and Rodrigo hesitated, judging the current's flow from where the horses stood to the black hole just beyond a clear white stretch of sandy beach. Then Rodrigo was in the water again, his horse's head raised, nostrils flared, and pulling steadily toward the opposite bank. Blake followed and the coldness closed about his chest once more.

They surged onto the beach and the horses stood with water running in coursing rivulets from their underbellies and dripping noiselessly onto the sand. Rodrigo moved toward the black hole and swung down, as did Blake.

Leading their horses, they saw the roots of a huge tree clutching at the sky like the fingers of a man being swallowed by quicksand. They left the horses in the shadow of the roots and moved forward into the blackness.

For untold years the winter rivers had probed and dug at the bank behind the gaint tree when it had stood, and now a cave, twice the height of a man standing, was carved into the sandstone. Rodrigo and Blake searched the inky blackness, each finding an opposite wall and working their way toward the rear. There was a slight bend in the cave and Rodrigo, on the short side, banged his shin against something and cursed softly in the darkness. Then he knelt and his hand touched the spokes of a wheel. Like a blind man identifying a friend's face, his hands worked along the wagon until they touched the crates in the back.

"Blake!" The word urgent but whispered.

"Yeah, Rod?" came from somewhere in the consuming blackness.

"I found the wagon. The crates are all here. Let's get back to the trees."

"Right behind you."

They turned and felt their stumbling way toward the moonlight. Sand replaced the hard earth beneath their feet and they took up the reins to their horses and led them cautiously from the shadows and toward the river. Then the crickets ceased their clacking hum and frogs croaked once before plopping into the water. All was silent except for the whisper of the river—and the jangle of bit chains and the metallic click of saber against thigh.

## Chapter Eleven

Colonel Bibby refreshed his glass before going to the window to stare out at the parade ground, ghostly now in the full moonlight. He counted the troopers standing before their mounts again, even though he knew exactly how many there were. He turned toward Captain Stearns.

"Why such a small detachment, Captain? That's what I can't understand. If you think there is any chance at all of recovering those rifles, I want you to take every trooper that can walk, crawl or hobble to get the job done."

Stearns smiled, easing the glove onto his left hand with patient tugs. "Because we aren't certain that the rifles are where we think they are. Sergeant Elliot found the tracks of Mexican-shod horses along the river today. The tracks of several horses which seemed to be concentrated mostly near the big bend. I'm just playing a hunch here, hoping they will come back tonight and, with luck, lead us to the location of the stolen weapons."

Bibby waved the glass in the air and frustration showed florid on his face. "Then that's all the more reason to take the whole blessed fort! Hell, I'll even lead the damned thing myself if I have to!"

"That won't be necessary, Colonel, but thank you. Too large a force might scare them off, if they do come. You make sure that Lieutenant Ashford does as I instructed him to do. Have the lieutenant take one hundred troopers and leave in exactly forty-five minutes. Half his troops are to fan out in a firing line in the foothills breasting Little Poison Lake, and the other half are to remain mounted at the southern end of the ridge as a flanking unit. If these men are Mexicans and do have contraband U.S. weapons, they will use the salt beds going south to make the quickest possible time. We will take them in the narrow stretch of land between the foothills and Little Poison."

Stearns paused and Bibby winced at the cold deadliness that came over his face. "Tell Ashford that, if he sees a wagon approach and being pulled by six mules, to open fire when they are in range. It will be the men who killed my troopers. I will circle back and lead the flanking unit. It was my men who were killed. Good men. Rough, but good. And they were killed without mercy. There will be no mercy this time, either."

Startled by the cold-blooded look on the captain's face, Bibby drank quickly and turned away to hide his fright. "Certainly, Captain, you are absolutely correct. Excellent military strategy." His knuckles went against his spine again and he turned cautiously, careful of balance. "I want those weapons, Captain Stearns. And I want those two men who escaped. And I want the whole kit and kaboodle dropped into Juárez's lap. After that, I don't give a damn."

Stearns smiled cruelly. "And those two men dead would save us a hanging, wouldn't it, Colonel? And the chance that something else might go wrong?"

Bibby's head jerked and the chins bobbed furiously. "Dead, alive or gutshot, I want this damned mess settled!"

"I thought you would see it my way, Colonel," Stearns said, striding toward the door.

Bibby raised his hand in a half-salute, then let it drop as the captain hurried from the room. He looked at his hand questioningly, then steered it toward the bottle.

Captain Stearns and Sergeant Elliot rode side by side, and the other five riders ranged behind with no thought given to formation. Stearns talked just loudly enough to be heard as they set a course for the river.

"We'll do exactly as planned. After the exchange is made, Wayne, you and Thatcher will take the packhorse with the money and ride to Twin Buttes. I have a room rented above the saloon with a rear entrance—room number four. The rest of us will circle back and join the main command at Little Poison. You two stay with the money in the room until tomorrow afternoon when Luke and I will go into town on official military business." He paused, smiling in the moonlight. "That being to arrange accommodations for Colonel Bibby on the next available stage. By then he'll have the rifles, two dead bandidos, and I'll give him my personal assurance that the rifles will be delivered to Juárez."

Elliot looked across. "Are you actually going to give the rifles to that damned Mexer?"

"Sure, why not? I couldn't care less which side wins their miserable war. We'll have our fifteen thousand, and it's the only way to get rid of Bibby. When we get to the river, we'll rendezvous with Dubois and take him and the skinners to the south side of the cave. Six strong mules should be able to pull the wagon up that bank, and they don't need to worry about tracks like we did."

Rodrigo and Blake froze in their tracks. The jangle of metal and thud of hooves became louder, and they moved into the shadow of the fallen tree. They knew they were trapped, and draping their gun belts around their necks, they leveled their rifles toward the lesser slope and waited.

The horses came closer and Blake knew for sure he would never leave the riverbank alive. Resolve closed off his mind and he aimed his rifle at a spot where the bank contrasted with the sparkling galaxies. The clatter of hooves was nearly upon them now and Blake saw a silhouette fill his front sight. His finger tightened on the trigger, and he hoped it was Luke Wyler. The cold black hatred was there again, and he nestled the stock more comfortably against his shoulder. The hammer hung precariously on a slim bit of metal and the firing pin waited to slam a bullet down the barrel, but the horses turned away and paralleled the river. Blake let the sight touch on each of the passing riders and watched them pass from view and moonlight fill the void.

Rodrigo touched Blake's elbow lightly and pointed toward the crossing upstream. With his finger inching from the trigger, Blake lowered the rifle and looked in the direction of Rodrigo's hand. Twenty riders, some wearing sombreros, some not, sat in their saddles at the crossing. Six mules and a packhorse with canvas sacks strapped to its back stood patiently by on lead ropes.

"What the hell's going on?" Blake hissed, his tone low but urgent.

Rodrigo remained silent, watching, calculating, and when he spoke, he did so without taking his eyes off the mounted unit.

"It's Maximilian's men."

"How do you know that?"

"The French always wear those ridiculous hats. Quickly, Blake. Into the water. The current will sweep us around the bend and out of sight. We'll join Munn and the others and circle back behind them."

Blake slipped into the cold wetness and the soaked coat dragged him down in the swirling current. His hand slipped on the saddle horn and he struggled to hold his weapons high while his boots sucked him deeper into the black depths. The horse found the sandbar and the toes of Blake's boots dragged through the soft mud. He scrambled for a better hold and his grip was firm around the horn as the horse went under again, lashing with the powerful drive of its hooves toward the opposite shore.

His left arm was tiring and his legs ached and his grip loosened on the slick saddle horn again. The dark mass of trees was but twenty yards away now, but to Blake they might have been miles. His heart pounded in his chest and he knew he could hold on no longer. The horse surged upward and Blake lost his grip, but his boots touched bottom and he stood neck-deep in the swirling backwash. At the last second, he grasped the tip of the horse's tail and the plunging animal dragged him up the bank. He fell to his knees in the tall grass with sides heaving in great gasps while a weak trembling passed through his thighs.

Rodrigo rode toward him with his gun belt dangling from his saddle horn. "Can you ride, Blake?"

"Yeah. Yeah, sure. Just . . . just let me catch my breath a second."

Blake's horse had wandered a few yards away and Rodrigo caught the animal and led it back. Struggling to his feet, Blake strapped on his gun belt and stabbed for a stirrup with a water filled boot. Finally, he swung wearily into the saddle and fell in behind Rodrigo as he moved into the trees.

Munn and the others were mounted and waiting when Blake and Rodrigo neared the edge of the grove. Munn pointed toward the crossing where two groups stood facing each other with rifles ready but not aimed. Two mounted riders were silhouetted between them, one wearing a French block cap and the other a cavalry hat. Then the two men turned their horses and rode along the bank to the sloping approach to the cave and dismounted. Torches were lit and they entered the cave. Ghostly shadows flickered in the mouth of the cave and Blake could see the Frenchman stoop over the wagon, count the cases, and pry the top off one to examine the rifles.

"Are we going to take them?" Blake asked, leaning toward Rodrigo. The weariness was gone and had been replaced by determination.

"No. Not now, anyway. There are twenty-seven of them, twenty-nine counting the two in the cave. We will have to wait for our chance."

"But what if the Frenchman heads for the border with your rifles? It will still be twenty against nine. If he gets to the border the rifles will be lost."

Rodrigo's eyes narrowed as he watched the flickering torches. "One card at a time, Blake. One card at a time."

The inspection completed, the Frenchman went to the mouth of the cave and waved his torch in a circle. He waited, waved it twice more, then once again. The skinners moved forward with the mules and one of the riders in a Mexican sombrero took up the reins of the packhorse. The mules brayed loudly in the eerie stillness as they stepped lock-shouldered down the sloping bank. Skilled hands quickly hooked them to the traces and the wagon rolled toward the mouth of the cave with a mighty groan.

The snap of bull whips and the grinding sound of lunging hooves drifted across the river as the wagon inched its creaking way up the bank and paused on the crest before turning toward the crossing. The two commanders rode in the lead and approached the packhorse. Torches were lit again, the sacks were opened, the money counted and inspected, then the flares were tossed into the river with a dying hiss. The two leaders saluted each other and the wagon with its escorts turned toward the south.

When the wagon was out of earshot, a deep, rumbling, exultant scream split the night sky. Blake stared toward the seven riders yet at the crossing and hatred seared his brain. He knew the voice, and the man from whom it had come. His hands worked impatiently at the cold metal of the Winchester in his grasp.

Rodrigo was looking in the direction the wagon had gone and Blake whispered across dejectedly, "We've lost the rifles, Rod."

The black sombrero turned and Rodrigo smiled. "No we haven't, Blake my friend. Not yet we haven't."

The small group at the crossing mounted up and two riders, leading the pack animal, moved into the river while the other five wheeled their horses and raced along the bank in the direction from which they had come. Blake could sense the tenseness in Rodrigo and Munn as they watched the two unsuspecting riders ford the river then turn toward the outer edge of the grove at a leisurely gallop.

Rodrigo's eyes flashed to Munn's face and the gypsy nodded. Slipping the loop of the bola from his saddle horn, he jumped from the saddle and moved silently into the forest to be quickly swallowed by the darkness. Rodrigo was not five seconds behind. Two minutes went by before the lead rider swung his horse to clear the outermost tree. The second man was ten yards behind, his rifle in the crotch of his arm and head swinging from side to side warily. Then he too swung wide to clear the tree.

It came up instantly, a faint whir like the rising of a startled flock of mountain quail. The second rider straightened in the saddle for the briefest moment, ramrod stiff before toppling to one side. The horse continued to run with reins lying loose on its neck. The lead rider whirled an instant before he, too, slammed from the saddle.

A gigantic object rushed from the trees, stooped, hesitated and moved backward. A second, smaller silhouette moved forward, hunched down and dragged the other soldier toward the grove.

Blake urged his horse through the timber and the others followed. Munn loomed in the darkness and his gold teeth glinted in the moonlight like a cat's eyes. He pointed down at his feet at the unconscious soldier lying there with the thongs of the bola still wrapped around his neck.

"Is he dead?" Blake asked.

Munn shook his head and stooped to loosen the thongs. He slapped the soldier on either cheek and forced him to a sitting position while drawing his knife and pressing its tip against the jugular vein. The soldier blinked his eyes, rubbed his head and looked up. Rodrigo looked down, his face cold and expressionless.

The other trooper lay motionless on the ground. Stepping down, Blake knelt beside him and unwound the leather straps from around his neck. He rolled the soldier onto his back and a startled gasp escaped his lips. He stared at the young trooper, frozen in his stooped position and Rodrigo moved to Blake's side.

"He isn't dead, Blake, unless he broke his neck in the fall."

Blake's lips moved in soundless damnation and his hands

moved toward the bruised throat. Rodrigo's firm grip closed about Blake's wrists and pulled his hands away.

"He is of no use to us dead. Your chance will come later," the Argentinian said, studying Blake's face closely. "Is he one of them?"

Blake nodded, but his eyes never left the young soldier's face. "Yes. His name is Wayne Wyler. He's the youngest of the three."

"Excellent. We have a bigger prize than I had hoped for. Now, collect their horses; it will take your mind off things while we bind and gag these two. We will take them to the arroyo, and Hank can watch over them while we go after the wagon."

As they approached the arroyo they heard the solid click of a hammer coming to full cock, followed by a lever action snapping open and shut and they reined in their horses a safe distance away. Blake grinned at Rodrigo before cupping his hands to his mouth.

"Hank! It's me, Blake! We've brought home a couple of scorpions for you to baby-sit!"

Silence in the narrow walled canyon. After nearly a minute, they heard a voice. "Yeah? Let me hear Munn say something!" the voice challenging, uncertain. Biggie Munn laughed his sucking laugh and a chuckle drifted from the arroyo. "Okay. Come on in!"

The two soldiers were conscious now and staring at the floor of the canyon, strapped as they were across their saddles.

The Mexicans quickly unlashed them and dragged the two men to a sitting position against the wall opposite Hank. Munn kindled a tiny fire and weak light licked dark fingers on the walls. Hank eyed the two men and a huge grin split his face.

"Well, if it ain't Corporal Thatcher and Corporal Culhane come a-callin'. Same two fellers who saw me ambush an army wagon. Ain't this a coincidence now? I think it's face bustin' time."

Wayne Wyler's hating eyes had been on Hank until Blake

stepped into the firelight. "Not that one, Hank," Blake said, jerking a thumb toward Wyler. "He's mine all the way."

Hank's eyes narrowed and his face twisted. "He one of 'em?"

"Yes. His name's Wayne Wyler."

"That makes him double special interesting."

Rodrigo moved forward and lashed the two men back to back while Munn led the packhorse deeper into the canyon. "Hank, keep an eye on these two until we get back. Some of Maximilian's men are heading south right now with our rifles, and we're going to have to catch them before daylight." He nodded toward the direction the pack animal had gone before taking up the reins to his horse. "That packhorse might be of some interest to you as well. I'd guess it's wearing at least ten, maybe fifteen thousand dollars."

Hank looked down the arroyo again. "Always did like speckled horses. That one in particular." He glanced up at the men standing before him. "Better get goin', fellers. It must be damned near midnight. Don't worry about these two lads here, and for sure, don't worry about that packhorse."

Blake smiled and watched Hank's eyes. "It's not the horse we're worried about, Hank. It's you."

"Yeah, well you worry about me while you're catching those rifles, and I'll worry about me sittin' here with my foot about to fall off! Now get the hell out of here! Some of us got work to do!"

Riding hard but cautiously, keeping the high ground between them and the desert floor, two hours passed before they pulled in at the edge of a rimrock and looked down. The wagon was nearing the bluffs opposite Little Poison Lake, with five riders in front led by the French cap; five were to the rear and the others ranged on either side.

Rodrigo pointed toward the jagged, raised ground which created a two-hundred-yard-wide channel between the buttes and the lake. "We're too late," he said softly. "I had hoped to take them there. Better find another place before dawn. Let's move."

They hadn't gone twenty yards before fifty explosions ripped the dry air. Horses whirled on churning hooves and fought tight reins in panic. Yellowish-orange muzzle blasts dotted the buttes, and the jarring crash of repeating rifles fired at random flooded across the desert and reverberated off the rimrock.

Blake felt the hair rise on the back of his neck and waited for the awful stinging thud of a bullet as he scrambled to leap clear of the saddle. But when his feet hit the ground and he joined the others in the relative safety provided by a huge outcropping of rock, there had been no whining cry of bullets searching out their victims in the darkness.

Blake eased up beside Rodrigo. "If they're shooting at us, Rod, they're damned poor shots."

Rodrigo listened to the continuing fusillade. "They aren't."

"Well, if they aren't shooting at us, who the hell is shooting at who?"

Rodrigo's face was drawn tight and he nodded toward the edge of the rimrock. "I think I know, but let's find out for sure."

Inching along belly down on the yet warm rocks, they crept forward to the ledge of the rimrock. When they looked down, the sight below sickened them to a man.

A steady barrage of rifle fire, now staccato, ripped from the high ground. There were ten empty saddles below and those yet alive fired from their plunging horses at targets unseen. The man in the French cap leaped onto the wagon, pushed the two dead mule skinners from the seat, and whipped the reins across the backs of the team now kicking and braying in their traces. The wagon moved forward again several yards before the off-lead mule lunged above the others, faltered and sagged to the ground. Its body weight dragged the other lead mule down in a thrashing heap and the wagon stopped.

Seven escort riders remained now and one swept past the wagon with a riderless horse. The Frenchman leaped onto the mount and snatched the reins just before a bullet slammed into his chest. The horse's head came up and around at a full gallop and both horse and rider sprawled across the desert floor. When the horse regained its senses, it stood and staggered away but the Frenchman was motionless and his hat flopped once in a gust of wind.

The remaining escort riders milled about in wild confusion, their horses panicked and nearly uncontrollable. A short, squat Mexican took command and spurred his horse in headlong flight for the open land beyond the buttes. Lowered in saddles and hugging withers, the others followed. The rifle fire stopped from the high ground, and Blake looked down in stunned amazement.

"Thank God," he said almost breathlessly, "at least some of them will get away."

Rodrigo's face was rigid, like chiseled stone, and the negative shake of his head was but the slightest movement. He pointed toward the fleeing riders and Blake looked again toward Little Poison Lake.

Fifty troopers on rested mounts spurred toward the lake from the far point of the ridge and fanned out in a battle line, cutting off the escorts and firing as they galloped toward the wagon and closing off the southern retreat. Two more riders flopped to the ground and the others wheeled their horses in a desperate attempt to retrace their route and escape to the north. But they had to pass beneath the rifles from above to gain their freedom, and when they were in range a merciless, rattling sheet of steel rained down upon them. In an instant, five horses and their riders lay dead upon the sandy soil.

A sickening gurgle surged through Blake's stomach. He laid his head on his forearms and his face was wet with sweat even though the night was cold. Then he heard the laugh and his head jerked up. Even from that distance, he recognized the big sergeant riding beside his captain.

Captain Stearns rode casually among the fallen. Several men moaned and writhed upon the ground and Stearns turned his horse to face the mounted cavalry.

"Listen up, men!" His strong voice carried in the still desert air. "These are the scum that killed sixteen of your comrades! They killed them from ambush and left no survivors! There was no mercy given, no compassion felt. And I say, an eye for an eye! Sergeant Elliot! Take a patrol of ten men and put a bullet through the head of each bandit, alive or dead! Corporal Butler? Cut the lead team free from the wagon! The remaining four can pull it to the fort, and throw two bodies in the back!"

The kill-shots were spaced, random blasts muffled by the target itself. First there were nineteen shots, a terrible pause, and finally the twentieth. The two bodies closest to the wagon were dumped in like sack potatoes and the corporal scrambled onto the seat. The fifty troopers from the high ground, now mounted, came down in formation and took up positions at the head of the wagon while those from the flanking maneuver took up the rear. Captain Stearns and Sergeant Elliot moved to the head of the column and the wagon creaked and rattled toward the fort.

The men watching from the rimrock were silent for long moments. Blake breathed deeply, and it felt good to have air in his lungs again and to feel his heart beating in his chest. Finally, he glanced over at the man beside him whose eyes had not left the carnage below.

"Stearns is an animal, Rod," Blake said simply.

"Yes," Rodrigo agreed, his words soft and distant. "There are many in uniform who are animals."

Blake watched the wagon disappear and he felt a sad, heavy depression in his chest. "We had the rifles within our grasp twice tonight and lost them both times."

Rodrigo nodded.

"What are we going to do now?"

Rodrigo looked across and there was a tight smile on his face. "We have only played two cards, Blake. There are three left. I don't think Stearns and Elliot will forget their gun money easily. "Come," he said, rising heavily to his feet and moving toward the horses, "it will be necessary for Benito to know who the Frenchman was."

They rode slowly toward the crumpled, dark heaps stretched lifeless on the sand. The Frenchman, with his hand outstretched toward his cap, remained where he had fallen. Rodrigo stepped down and turned the man onto his back with gentle hands. He nodded as he looked down at the broken face.

"Marcel Pierre Dubois."

"Did you know him?" Blake asked.

"Yes, I knew him. We have fought many battles, he and I. He was a brave and worthy opponent, and one who would never have shot the wounded. That would have been left to the jackals. His death, by the hand of whomever, is our gain. But, it should never have come this way." Rodrigo bowed his head, crossed himself and stepped back into the saddle. He took one last look at the Frenchman before turning his horse's head. "I don't believe in prayers, but perhaps he did," Rodrigo said quietly. "The dead and those dying must believe in something."

## Chapter Twelve

Colonel Bibby heard the sentry's call and scurried from his office. The yellow glow of coal-oil lamps was muted in that moment of sullen gray between when the moon falls and the sun rises. His step was slightly unsteady and, remembering, he paused to light his cigar.

"Open the gates!" Bibby commanded with bellowing authority.

"Yes, sir!"

Two troopers threw back the drawbar and pulled the heavy gates aside. Bibby moved into the center of the parade ground and peered into the morning gloom. He could see the long column strung out across the desert, but as yet, he could see no wagon. He ran first to one side and then the other to the limit of vision the walls would allow, but still could see no wagon. "Damn," he muttered, waiting for the slow-moving horses to draw near.

The captain and sergeant were the first to enter, and Stearns saluted smartly while Elliot attempted a half-hearted poke at his hat brim. Bibby stood frozen, watching the weary troops enter and refusing to budge until he saw the wagon, any wagon.

When the first mule entered, Bibby's face brightened like a mirror held to a lamp. The front wheels rolled by and the colonel rushed forward. Mindless of the rear wheels, he grabbed the sideboards and heaved his bulk up for a peek. The darkened crates were there, heavy and silent. He reached out to touch them, just to be sure, and his hand touched a cold, blood-matted face. Bibby lurched backward, falling, then scrambling on hands and knees to clear the rear wheels.

Bibby retrieved himself from the dust and his eyes found Captain Stearns again. He was terrified of the man, proud of him and relieved all in the same instant while his hand unconsciously worked against a pants leg in an attempt to wipe away the strange coldness.

Stearns dismissed the troops and swung slowly down, and handing his horse to a private, he disappeared into his quarters followed by Sergeant Elliot. Bibby took two hesitant steps across the parade ground before catching himself. Military pride intervened, and he turned back toward his office with dejection diminishing his already economical steps.

Bibby was seated behind his desk and contemplating the empty glass before him when the door swung open and banged against the wall. Captain Stearns stepped inside and kicked the door closed while removing the leather gloves from his fingertips with studied concentration. His expression was blank and Bibby offered a weak, testing smile. Stearns rapped his gloves sharply on the colonel's desk before leaning forward on his knuckles. His face was cold and deadly, as though there had not been enough death to satiate his appetite. Finally he allowed a cautious smile to form on his handsome face.

"Too early for a little victory drink, Colonel?"

Bibby scrambled to his feet and bounded toward the bottle.

"Not on your life, Captain! Not on your life!" He poured generously and the glasses trembled only slightly in his hands as he handed one to the captain. "To you, sir! And to a glorious victory!"

Stearns nodded, continuing to smile, his eyes watching Bibby as the glass came to his lips. Bibby held the gaze as long as he could before glancing away and puffing into his version of what a military rooster should look like. He strutted a dauntless pace across the office and turned when he felt the distance was as safe as space would allow.

"Tell me about it, Captain. Please, sit and tell me about it. I only wish I could have been there to lead the second assault, but as you wisely suggested, a commander's place is to command, not to execute." He grinned sheepishly. "Or words to that effect."

Stearns drew up a chair and draped a leg over a corner of the colonel's desk. "It went like clockwork, Colonel. Like a finely tuned Swiss watch. I had the small detachment take up positions near where we felt the weapons were hidden. They came late in the night, twenty bandidos and six mules. We waited until we had positive confirmation of their direction of travel, which was toward Little Poison Lake, as I suggested. Then I took my men, following a circuitous route which, given the pace of a heavily laden wagon, I knew would allow me time to reach the mounted command and lead the flanking maneuver. Lieutenant Ashford had his troops in perfect position in the hills, and when he called for the bandits to stop, they commenced to fire. Ashford had no choice and our troops returned the volley with great accuracy, and great bravery, I might add." Stearns sipped his drink and watched the colonel. "I was wrong in what I said earlier, Colonel. You've kept these troops in fighting trim, sir."

Bibby blushed and nearly choked on his whiskey. He coughed once, pounded his chest, coughed again and regained a semblance of control. "Well, thank you, ah, Captain. Yes . . . I am quite a stickler for combat readiness." He turned quickly to hide the shock in his eyes. "But that's not important. Go on, tell me more."

Stearns smiled at the colonel's sloping shoulders. "They tried to make a run for it, but I was waiting for their cowardice and out-maneuvered them. The flanking movement was executed flawlessly, they had nowhere to go. But, I'm sorry to say, there were no survivors. They fought to the end. On the bright side, however, we suffered not one casualty, not so much as a broken thumb nail."

Bibby turned, beaming. "Beautiful, Captain. Absolutely perfect. And the weapons? Have they been tampered with?"

"Not at all. They are in the same condition as they were when I left the Midwest with them."

Now Bibby's face dimmed and he studied the whiskey. "About those two who escaped. I was instructed to bring them to justice before I could get the hell out . . . ah, er, have to give up my command. Did you . . ."

"They have been brought to justice, Colonel," Stearns said somberly. "The only kind of justice they know, at any rate. They are dead, in the back of the wagon now as a matter of fact." He made as if to rise. "Would you care to make a positive identification, or can you accept my word?"

Bibby rushed forward and gently pushed the captain down. "No, that won't be necessary. Your word is more than sufficient with me. Just have them buried quickly, this morning if possible."

"As good as done. One more thing, Colonel. Sergeant Elliot and I will be going into Twin Buttes this afternoon to make certain arrangements." Stearns looked up innocently. "If they are still in your plans, that is."

"Definitely, Captain. Most definitely. Even though I regret leaving, I'll have to admit I'm rather anxious to be going. When one's work is finished, there is no point in lingering unduly, is there? I have a most capable replacement, a man deserving of his own command, and I can leave here knowing no problems will close on my wake, if you'll excuse an old army man the use of a nautical term."

Bibby moved with a near fluid grace now, as though twenty pounds and an equal number of years had been magically removed from his body. "I'll rough out a wire saying that everything is under control, the outlaws are dead, that the weapons have been recovered and will be delivered by you personally to Juárez. You will make certain of the transfer of those rifles?"

"Of course I will, sir."

"Fine. Then when you go in to make reservations for me on that stage, there's one leaving three days hence, I . . . I kinda checked on that, if you'd just pop by the telegraph office and get that little nuisance off my back, I can relax and enjoy my last few days at Fort Hastings."

Stearns took a final drink and placed the glass carefully on Bibby's desk before moving toward the door. "Consider it done, sir. If you could just have your orderly bring that message to my quarters this afternoon around two o'clock, I will be prepared to deliver it personally for you. Right now, I'm going to get some sleep."

"Very good, Captain. And have a nice rest, you deserve one. An honest day's work makes for pleasant dreams, as they say."

Stearns grinned broadly from the doorway. "You're the man who would know about that, sir. Good morning, Colonel."

When the door closed, Colonel Bibby would have leaped into the air and clicked his heels together if it had been in his power to do so. As it was, he settled for finishing off the captain's whiskey.

## Chapter Thirteen

Rodrigo poured a cup of coffee and leaned against the wall of the arroyo. The rising sun touched the tips of the canyon wall, the shadows crept slowly downward and a vulture glided effortlessly overhead in a southerly direction. He sipped his coffee and looked at the two men, still bound and gagged, across from him.

"Did our guests give you any trouble during the night, Hank?" Rodrigo asked.

Hank looked up from the boot he was trying to work onto his injured foot. "Nope. But then they didn't say a hell of a lot, and they stuck pretty close together."

Blake watched Hank wince as he went back to work on the boot. "How's it feeling?"

"Like shovin' your fist into a bear's mouth."

Blake laughed, but he could feel Wayne Wyler's eyes on his back. Turning, he refilled his cup and smiled coldly.

"Howdy, Wayne."

Wyler stared at Blake and his eyes were twin dots of hatred.

Rodrigo indicated Wyler with his cup. "Take the gag off, Blake. Certainly your old friend would like to have a chat with you."

Blake whipped the gag from Wyler's mouth and stepped back. He could feel the hatred rising and tried to force it from his mind.

"I said, howdy, Wayne. Damned unpleasant surprise seeing you again."

Wyler worked his mouth, stretching the muscles and arching his neck. "How 'bout a drink of water," he said sullenly.

Rodrigo shook his head. "Water will come later. After we've talked."

Wyler stared contemptuously at Rodrigo before looking at Blake. "What are you doing here, Evans?"

"Come to join the army. Hear they're takin' just about anybody now."

"Not a bad life once you get used to it," Wyler countered with a curling grin.

"No, I suppose not. Perfect place for a cold-blooded killer."

Wyler's face hardened again and he stared at the far wall. Rodrigo rolled a cigarette, lit it and leaned forward slightly.

"Who is Captain Stearns?"

Implacable, Wyler continued his stare.

Rodrigo smiled casually and shrugged his shoulders. "Take the gag off the other one, Blake, please."

Blake removed the bandanna and the soldier moistened his lips and worked his jaw.

"What's your name?" Rodrigo asked, almost cordially.

"Corporal Purvis Thatcher!" he snapped, his eyes staring straight at Rodrigo.

"Who is your commanding officer?"

"Captain Mathew Stearns, United States Cavalry."

"Captain Stearns?" Rodrigo mused. "I met him one time. Real gentleman."

Blake thought he saw Thatcher's eyes waver then correct themselves.

"He is that."

"Correction. He was, but he isn't now." Rodrigo's voice became a cutting edge. "Because the real Captain Stearns is dead, and your Captain Stearns is the scum of the earth. What's his real name?"

"Stearns. Captain Mathew Stearns."

"I see. Where are you from originally, Corporal Thatcher?"

"Charleston, West Virginny . . . ah, West Virginia."

"I don't know American geography very well. Is that in the North or the South?"

"We fought for the North, if that's what you mean."

"That's what I mean." Rodrigo watched Thatcher in silence for several moments. "You know, Thatcher, I think you really are a soldier. Or were. With which unit did you fight during the war?"

Thatcher concentrated, and his eyes definitely wavered this time. Blake watched the interrogation in amazement.

"Am I a prisoner of war?"

"No. Just a prisoner."

"Then I don't have to tell you a goddamned thing!"

Rodrigo smiled without humor. "No, perhaps you don't. But you will." He drained his coffee cup and leaned against the wall with a heavy sigh. He looked at either man and their eyes were upon him with cautious uncertainty. Rodrigo shrugged. "Torture is a barbarous thing at best. It is cruel, often fatal and always unpleasant, and I would like to avoid that unpleasantness if at all possible. But I have no choice in the matter, unfortunately. I need information. You have information to give. It is as simple as that. If you are to avoid the pain of torture, you will have to comply with my wishes. If you decide not to, then I am left with no other choice. A very simple equation. Which will it be?"

The two men watched Rodrigo in sullen hostility and gave no indication of acceptance or rejection.

Rodrigo held his hands up in a gesture of helplessness. "What am I to do?" he asked, turning toward the entrance to the arroyo. "Munn?"

Biggie Munn's massive frame blocked the sunlight and he moved toward them with long, athletic strides. He held in his hands an earthenware jar and a stick with a thin, wire hoop on one end.

Hank had given up the struggle with his boot and sat watching with a sock stretched over his swollen left foot. Rodrigo waited until Munn placed the jar carefully on the ground before turning to Hank.

"Take your sock off, Hank, and show our guests your foot."

Puzzled, Hank dragged the sock free and held his leg up.

The puffed, yellow-black foot appeared as though it might have been dragged from the bottom of a swamp. The skin throbbed with fresh blood pounding through it and Hank's toes quivered in response to pain.

"Thank you, Hank," Rodrigo said, his eyes going back to the two captives. "That was the result of the sting from a single scorpion less than sixteen hours ago. One single scorpion, mind you."

He nodded toward Munn who lifted the lid from the jar and held his hoop poised deftly over the opening before stabbing down. He worked the stick carefully for breathless seconds before grinning and pulling the hoop from the jar. With the wire encircling its upper body, snaring the animal just behind its front claws, the large, ugly black scorpion lashed with its tail and squirmed to be free. The tail came up, held in a deadly arch, then snapped down again. The angry animal sagged against the hoop and raised its tail a third time.

Rodrigo waved his hand and Munn lowered the scorpion back into the jar and replaced the lid.

Thatcher and Wyler stared at the jar and their eyes rolled in horror. Wyler's face trembled and Thatcher's lips twitched, and sudden sweat rolled down their faces.

"As I said," Rodrigo began again, "torture is an unpleasant business, and one which can be avoided. There are ten scorpions in that jar, five apiece. Their sting is most painful, and deadly, on the flat of the stomach. Worse than a knife blade, as a matter of fact. You will be separated and stretched upon the ground, bare to the waist. One scorpion will be added for each question unanswered truthfully and correctly. You can stop the punishment whenever you choose, simply by co-operating. Or, by the same means, you can prevent it from occurring in the first place." He watched them almost like a father scolding his sons. "Which will it be?"

With the scorpion out of sight, Thatcher regained his control, but Wayne Wyler continued to stare at the jar and the spasmodic twitches increased along his jaw.

"Purvis . . . I . . . I think he means it," Wyler managed, his lips barely moving.

Thatcher's head snapped toward the pathetic voice. "Shut up, Wayne! Damnit, shut up!" He looked at Rodrigo and his head shook slowly in disbelief. "You wouldn't do that sort of thing to a man. It ain't human."

"True, it isn't. But shooting wounded men in the back of the head is even less human. You, and people like you, have abrogated your right to be treated as humans."

Rodrigo turned toward the Mexicans standing silently nearby and snapped a command. They quickly untied the two prisoners, jerked them to their feet and stripped away their uniform shirts. Three of the Mexicans led Wyler to the far end of the arroyo while the other three stretched Thatcher out before Rodrigo. Munn divided the scorpions, placing five in a separate jar, and handed it to Blake.

Blake looked up in stunned surprise, and the jar in his hands felt like it was crawling. He held it away while glancing frantically at Rodrigo. Rodrigo acknowledged the glance, but his face was impassive as leather. He took up a second stick and spoke without looking at Blake.

"You will have to do Wyler, Blake. Munn can't ask questions. He'll handle the scorpions, you get the information. Who is Stearns? Where did he come from? What are they going to do with the rifles now? Where was the money to be picked up? And, most importantly, what is their overall plan? Munn will seal Wyler's ears, as I will this pig before me. I don't want them to be able to hear each other talk or one hear the screams of the other." He looked at Hank who had finally worked the boot onto his foot. "You go with him, Hank."

Hank stood and Blake automatically handed the jar toward him. Hank's hands snapped to his sides and he pointed at his left foot with a weak grin. "We already met."

Munn led the way with Hank and Blake following somewhat reluctantly behind. Wayne Wyler was lying upon the ground with a Mexican pinning either arm and one sitting on his legs. Munn pulled the bandanna from his neck and stooped as he fashioned it into long, neat folds. He packed the innermost fold with sand, interlaced the other folds over the top, then raised Wyler's head and tied the cloth around his head with the sand packs over his ears. Wyler stared up, his face nearly as white as his eyes. He tried to talk, but muttered only incoherencies instead. His stomach muscles twitched, glistening with sweat and his body writhed against the pressure.

Munn stood over him, took the jar from Blake's hands and probed inside the cool adobe.

Blake looked helplessly at Hank and Hank looked back. They hesitated, still standing, before Hank reached over and gently pushed Blake's shoulder down. "You go ahead, Blake. I can't remember the questions."

"Thanks," Blake mumbled, kneeling beside Wyler's head and turning to look at the massive gypsy. For the first time that he could remember, there was no humor in the blue eyes. It had been replaced by an opaque, vacant nothingness. A huge, more yellow than black scorpion squirmed and lashed at the end of the stick in his hand which was slowly lowering toward Wyler's twitching stomach.

Wyler lurched backward, eyes rolled up in terror, and his lips moved in a senseless babble.

Blake bent down and the scorpion inched closer to the soft white flesh. He glanced once at the vicious creature before speaking to Wyler.

"Wayne? Look, Wayne, all you've gotta do is tell me . . ."

Wyler's eyes rolled down, he saw the scorpion no more than the width of a man's hand from his stomach, the eyes went up again, he screamed and his head lolled to one side with the eyelids dropping slowly like the sinking of a summer sun.

Blake's head snapped toward the scorpion. It wiggled and squirmed just above Wyler's limp stomach with tail lashing, mean, hungry and vicious. He looked into Munn's eyes and the emptiness melted into glistening blue consciousness.

"I think he passed out," Blake said, turning toward Hank.

"Smart move. Don't think I could have enjoyed a helluva lot of that myself."

Munn placed the scorpion back into the jar and motioned for Blake to tell Rodrigo. Blake wondered momentarily why the hell Hank couldn't tell him but, rising quickly, he returned to the other end of the arroyo.

Thatcher lay stretched out on the ground with a sand-filled bandanna wrapped around his head and Mexicans holding each of his limbs. Rodrigo stood above him, stick in hand and lowering slowly. Looking into Rodrigo's eyes, Blake saw the same strange vacuum as had been in Munn's eyes, as though the Argentinian could not see the man at his feet and was functioning in a hypnotic trance. His lips moved and words came out, questioning words, but the voice was not the same. It was like something from the distant past, like a dream relived.

"Rod?"

The scorpion's descent stopped just above Thatcher's stomach and Rodrigo's eyes cleared when he looked at Blake.

"Wyler passed out. Didn't say anything."

Rodrigo nodded and the clouds filled his eyes again.

Blake watched Thatcher stare at the animal, his breathing coming in ruptured gasps and his stomach rising and falling in turbulent waves. Rodrigo pressed the scorpion an inch closer and its stinger touched the hair on Thatcher's navel.

"Who is Stearns?" Rodrigo asked, his voice distant but demanding.

Thatcher was afraid to breathe now and he held his stomach sucked deeply against his backbone. When he breathed again, the stinger would strike home.

"You have until your next breath to tell me." The voice vacant like the eyes.

Thatcher's eyes bulged and red veins popped out in the field of white.

"Okay. Okay," he whispered hoarsely, losing his remaining breath. "I'll tell you. But first, get that damned thing away from me!"

The scorpion was raised no more than two inches and Thatcher drew in a tortured cautious breath. Rodrigo waited, allowing the lungs to fill.

"Who is he?"

"Jason T. Burke," Thatcher said, looking away in self-disgust.

"Where is he from?"

"Virginia. All three of us are."

"You, Burke and who else?"

"Private Moody."

"Then you were in the Confederate Army?"

"Yup."

"Explain."

"Jason was our commanding officer, Moody and me that is. It was at the end of the war, the last major battle. We was all that was left of our unit. The war was over, and we knowed it. Ours and theirs was lying all over the place, wounded, dying or dead. We come across three blue legs lyin' face down in a ditch, shot in the back of the head. Jason come up with this idea, we swap uniforms and pass ourselves off as faithful Union soldiers from West Virginny. That'd explain the accent an' all." Thatcher paused, watching the scorpion now several inches from his stomach, and looked up at Rodrigo with a heavy sigh. "Could you put that thing away? I'm gonna tell it all to ya anyhow. I could use a smoke real bad."

Rodrigo straightened and a transformation came over his face. The eyes cleared and there was depth to them once again. He gently helped the corporal to his feet, rolled and lit a cigarette for him and handed over the wineskin.

"Here, rest a moment and relax. Have some wine, then continue."

Thatcher sucked greedily at the cigarette before gulping the wine in long, thirsty swallows. Purple ran down his cheeks and throat and onto his white chest but he seemed not to notice. Finally, he corked the skin, took a drag from the cigarette and spoke again.

"We took their identification papers, and in the confusion,

what with the war bein' over an' all, we pulled it off. Ole Jase was a colonel in our army, but the Yankee uniform he took belonged to a lieutenant. Anyway, we asked to be transferred immediately to the frontier."

"So when Captain Stearns was sent to take command of Fort Hastings, the three of you were sent with his detachment?"

"That's true for a fact. Jason's a damned good officer because he's mean. Smart mean. Killin' don't matter no more to him'n swattin' a fly. He likes two things, money and bein' a commanding officer, and what with our army bein' out of business, he decided to be a commanding officer in your army. He met the Wyler brothers in a saloon in New Mexico and they took up right off. Jase knew about the rifles we'd be escortin', and that they'd bring a high price in Mexico. He offered the Wylers in and they took to it like a cat to goldfish."

Thatcher paused for a drag from the cigarette and another squeeze from the wineskin and to study his story before continuing once more.

"It was perfect for us, till you fellers come along. The Wylers waited by a knoll near the river, and when we got there, old Jase was ridin' beside the captain. Me and Moody was back in the ranks. Jase eased his revolver out and had it laying across his lap. Then he squeezed the trigger and blew half the captain's chest off. Me and Moody threw down on the rest of 'em and Big Luke fired a couple of warning shots from the hill. Wasn't nothin' to it. We marched the rest of them bluelegs into a ravine, shot them and their horses, and spent the rest of the day coverin' 'em up."

Rodrigo's face was rigid and his lips were tight across his face as he spoke. "If I hadn't made an agreement with you, I'd give you back to the scorpions."

Thatcher grinned a dirty smile. "But you're a gentleman, see, and I ain't. That's a mighty important difference."

"Yes it is. Go on."

"Well, it was kinda like at the end of the war. Jase took the captain's identity, Big Luke the sergeant's and like that. Me?

Hell, I ain't Corporal Thatcher. I'm Orville J. Tully. Private, Army of the Confederacy."

"Okay, Tully. What are they going to do with the rifles now?"

"What they was supposed to do in the first place. Give 'em to that Juárez fella."

"What?" Rodrigo asked, unable to control his shock. "You said they are going to turn them over to Juárez?"

"Sure 'nuff for a fact. See, Jason can't take over command of the fort until them rifles is handed over proper 'cause Colonel Bibby can't leave till they are. So, we had to take 'em back last night. Plus, we needed a couple of dead bandits to take the place of these two," Tully said, nodding toward Hank and Blake.

Blake remembered the two dead escorts being dumped in the back of the wagon and knew their purpose now. Then he heard Rodrigo speak again.

"Where were you and Wyler going with the money last night?"

"Jason rented a room above the saloon, and we was goin' there to wait for him. He is supposed to come into town this afternoon to arrange for Bibby's stage fare."

"Why are you telling me all this in such great detail?" Rodrigo asked, squinting his eyes slightly.

"'Cause you still got them scorpions. I figure I'm a dead man anyway, but now maybe you'll do it with a gun or a knife instead of them godawful lookin' bugs."

"What was the room number?"

"Number four."

Rodrigo thought in silence for nearly a minute. "How would you like to live?" he asked, watching Tully's face.

"I'm mighty fond of that idea. Yes, sir, I am for a fact."

"Will you co-operate with me?"

"I'll co-operate with anybody what's got a knife at my throat. Name it and I'll do it."

"Fine. Get your shirt on."

Rodrigo motioned to Munn and the giant picked up the

earthenware jar and came from the far end of the ravine. He dumped the second into the first, then he followed Rodrigo to the entrance of the arroyo and stooped to listen to what was being said.

The Mexicans holding Wyler stood and hauled him to his feet. He staggered to the center of the ravine, his consciousness returning in greater measure with each step. A wild, crazed look filled his rolling eyes and he shivered as though standing in a frigid breeze. He stopped beside Tully, and the old veteran looked up at him.

"Sorry, son. I didn't have no choice but to tell 'em."

But Wyler was not listening. He stared at the earthenware jar sitting in the center of the ravine ten yards beyond and his body trembled. Sweat-streaked hair matted his forehead and his mouth twisted in utter revulsion.

"No!" he screamed, "don't put them on me. Please, don't put them on me!"

He sprang forward in a great lunge, and swinging his foot forward for a second stride, his boot caught on the tip of a rock. He stumbled forward, spraddle-legged, but his feet could not catch up with his plunging body. He sprawled head first to the ground and his chest smacked hard aga<u>nist</u> the earthenware jar. The shattering of the jar was nearly muffled by Wyler's screams as he slid to a stop, bare stomach down to the crushed adobe. Angry, the scorpions were quick to vent their rage.

Blake sat beneath the makeshift canopy at the top of the butte and stared at his boots. He heard the rattle of falling rock behind him, but he didn't look up as Rodrigo lowered himself into the wind depression. The Argentinian rolled a cigarette before handing the makings across. Blake shook his head and Rodrigo smoked in silence until Blake finally looked up.

"Would you have touched that scorpion to Tully's stomach, Rod?"

Rodrigo gazed at Blake through the drifting smoke. "Yes, I would have. If necessary."

"Why? That makes us the same as them, doesn't it?"

"In some ways."

"Then why?"

"For the same reason I was willing to leave Hank here. Because a million lives are worth more than one. By that same token, in a different situation, I would give my life to protect him."

"But, such a hideous torture, Rod? God, that was brutal."

"Torture is a means to an end, Blake. Honey in the eyes and tied to an ant hill? Cutting off one finger at a time? Stretching a man between two horses until he talks or breaks in half? I have seen such things done, and I doubt that you have. In any event, the captive has two distinct choices: talk or die."

"Why did you choose scorpions?"

"Because, as you said, it is a hideous death. So hideous, in fact, that few of the strongest men could endure the thought of it. Not the fact of dying itself, but the thought of dying in that manner. That is why I chose scorpions. I learned what I needed to know without touching stinger to flesh."

Blake wondered momentarily if he should ask the next thing on his mind, and then decided to. "I watched your eyes, and Munn's too, as you lowered the scorpion down. Something came over both of you. Something hypnotic, like you were in a trance. Did that same thing ever happen to you before?"

Rodrigo looked at Blake and the pupils of his eyes were dry and jet-black. "Yes. And neither of us talked."

Blake looked away, watching the sky beyond the edge of the canvas.

"It's a cruel world, isn't it, Rod?"

"No, the world isn't cruel. Nor are its natural creatures. But man is unnatural because of his cruelty. And he will be that way forever, Blake, because he is free of the necessity to kill to survive. He now kills for pleasure."

"Or for revenge."

"Yes, for revenge as well. But, if that revenge is justified the killing is not for pleasure or gain. It is because the heart bursts at the seams. Neither you nor I have ever killed for pleasure. But we will kill again. Because the sick ones will not allow us to live in peace."

Blake reached for his own makings and fashioned a smoke. "What will you do now? The rifles are at the fort, Tully has already confessed, and all you have to do is go in under a flag of truce and make your arrangements."

Smiling, Rodrigo struck a match and held it to Blake's cigarette. "It is not that simple, Blake. First, I offered Tully his life in exchange for information. That would be handing him to the hangman. Secondly, Burke would not stand idly by. And thirdly, there is the matter of the remaining Wyler brothers."

Blake glanced up in surprise. "The Wyler brothers? They're my problem, not yours."

"No, they are our problem. They jeopardized the future of my friend Benito Juárez, they have killed mercilessly, they led your brother to destruction and they would willingly have watched Hank hang. They are the vermin of the earth, the cruelty you spoke of. And we, the four of us, will settle our debt with them."

"How?"

Rodrigo sucked the last drag from his cigarette and ground it into the rock with his heel. He looked at Blake and his eyes were again filled with that deep, fathomless mystery.

"We will send their brother to them," he said softly and walked toward the trail.

## Chapter Fourteen

Well fed, groomed and rested, the two spirited roan cavalry mounts cantered sideways at the noise from the street, and their reddish coats glistened in the afternoon sunlight. Resplendent in sparkling, crisp uniforms of bright yellow on blue, the officer and the sergeant were the picture of military authority and presence as they steered their mounts courteously through traffic. Stearns touched the brim of his hat politely to the ladies, and Elliot hunched his shoulders and spine in an attempted bow. They swung down before the telegraph office and highly polished boots glinted in the bright, clear air.

"Sergeant," Stearns said, his voice friendly but authoritative, "I have some business to attend to. If you would care to refresh yourself at the saloon, I'll join you there in half an hour."

"Yassir!" Elliot said, saluting as sharply as his thick hands and arms would allow before hurrying across the street. Stearns watched the sergeant's retreat and shook his head in patient dismay.

Stepping into the telegraph office, the captain copied the note from Colonel Bibby verbatim onto a telegraph sheet. He handed the slip of paper to the elderly man with a courteous nod, passed over a generous tip, and crossed to the stage office.

"Good morning, ma'am," he said to the young lady behind the counter.

She looked up at the handsome officer and a blush crept into her cheeks. She curtsied and Stearns stole the moment to study the hint of cleavage at the top of her dress. His eyes went to hers as she straightened and she smiled without embarrassment.

"Good morning, sir. Can I help you?"

"I certainly hope so. I would like to arrange accommodations for Colonel Nevis Bibby on the westbound stage. It leaves in two days, if I'm correct." He paused, smiling, feigning embarrassment. "Pardon me, I have failed to introduce myself. I am Captain Mathew Stearns. Colonel Bibby's replacement as commanding officer of Fort Hastings."

"Pleased to meet you, Captain Stearns," she replied, dipping into a tiny curtsy. "I'm Gloria Masters. My father is an agent for the stage line."

Stearns bowed from the waist with the hat sweeping an arc across his chest. "It's an honor to make your acquaintance, Miss Masters. It is Miss, isn't it?"

"Yes, it's still Miss," she said, repressing a nervous giggle.

Their eyes met and a silent message was conveyed before she broke off the gaze. "I haven't seen you in town before, Captain. When did you arrive?"

"Only a few days ago. Things have been kind of hectic and this is my first real visit to town."

"Well, in that case, let me be the first to welcome you to Twin Buttes. This won't be your last visit, I trust?" she asked, bending over the receipt book.

Stearns smiled inwardly at her brazenness and mentally compared her with the girls he had known in the South. She was equally as beautiful as they, but lacking their refinement. But then this is the frontier, he reminded himself, and desert blossoms are to be judged both for their availability as well as their fragrance. She glanced up once from writing the bill and caught Stearns' eyes again on the hint of femininity. She only smiled and went back to her writing.

"No, Miss Masters, I'm sure it will only be the first of many."

Signing the voucher, he pushed it toward her long, delicate fingers. His hand intentionally touched hers and he left it there a second longer than necessary before withdrawing. He noticed she had made no effort to move hers.

He smiled again and moved back a step. "Just send that voucher to the quartermaster at the fort. I'll make certain personally that it is taken care of without delay. And may I say, meeting you has been the nicest thing that's happened to me since coming to the Territory."

She managed her blush again. "Why, thank you, Captain. You're too kind. Good-bye."

Their eyes held and the deeply tanned skin on Stearns' face made the blond moustache and hair appear to be even more blond. Finally, he broke off the gaze. "Good day to you, Miss Masters."

He walked smartly from the office, conscious of his broad shoulders, narrow hips and muscular thighs under the tight blue trousers. On the sidewalk, he carefully placed the hat on his head, brushed back the thick hair on the nape of his neck and stepped onto the street. As he crossed to the saloon, he knew she would be watching. And when he pushed on the swinging door, he turned as though something had suddenly caught his attention. He saw a head turn in the stage office window and move away. He felt pleased, very pleased, and stepped into the saloon.

Sergeant Elliot was drinking alone at the end of the bar when Stearns stepped up and placed a boot on the foot rail.

"Get 'er done, Cap'n?"

"Yes. Everything is taken care of. Even a little matter I had been concerned about but could not resolve."

"What's that?"

"Nothing that concerns you, Sergeant. Just a matter between a beautiful lady and myself."

"Hah!" Elliot snorted. "The purty ones is more trouble'n they're worth."

"Wrong, Sergeant. If handled correctly, they are no trouble at all." The twinkle faded from the captain's eyes and they became serious. "Have you been up to check the room yet?"

"No. But, if Wayne said he'd be there, he'll be there. He

knows how to follow orders purty good. The flat side of a board taught him that when he was just a whelp."

Stearns nodded. "Too bad that tactic doesn't work in the military. Let's finish this drink, then go up . . ."

The twin doors slammed apart and a young boy burst into the saloon. He stood gasping in the dim light, searching the room. When he saw the two uniformed men at the end of the bar, he lunged toward them.

"Captain! Captain! You gotta come . . . you gotta come . . . 'cause . . ."

"Now hold on there, son," Stearns said, gently grasping the boy's shoulders. "Just get your breath and then tell me what's the matter."

The boy stooped to place his hands on his knees and sucked in several deep breaths. When he could speak again, he brushed the hair from his eyes and looked up at the tall captain. "I got one of your horses."

Stearns smiled down. "That's good, and I thank you. You haven't got one of my horses, but perhaps you do have one belonging to the army." He dug in his pocket for some change. "Just take it over to the livery and they'll take care of it until I . . ."

"You don't understand, Captain! It's not just a horse! There's a man tied to the saddle!"

Stearns bolted for the door, nearly knocking the boy down which Elliot did as he rushed by. The boy scrambled to his feet and scurried between the two big men as they stepped onto the boardwalk.

"There he is, sir," the boy said, pointing. "Just like I said. And I think he's . . . dead."

The cavalry mount stood on the street with head drooping into a water trough and reins touching the ground. Seated in the saddle, stiff in death, erect where he had been tied, a young soldier stared with sightless eyes at the wall beyond. His shirt had been pulled over his shoulders, the yellow bandanna hung limply from his neck and his stomach was a distorted mass of black, ugly lumps. His saber had been driven through a slip of paper which flopped gently in the mild breeze against the scabbard.

Sergeant Elliot's face was a twisted expression of shock and horror. "Oh, God," he mumbled, his lips barely moving. "Oh, God! That's my brother. That's my little brother, Wayne!"

Captain Stearns moved hard-eyed toward the horse, took the reins and patted the horse's neck while reaching slowly for the note. He jerked it free, started to read it, then shoved it into his pocket. He turned to the gathering crowd and selected two men.

"You two! Take this horse to the stable! Get Corporal Culhane down, gently, mind you, and take him to the doctor's place." His eyes swept over the remainder of the crowd and hatred concealed the instant fear in his mind. A lean young Mexican sat his horse in the shade of a building, but the captain paid him no mind. "We'll get the people responsible for this outrage, and when we do, you are all invited to a hanging. Now, please clear the streets and go on about your business. This is an army matter and the army will handle it."

Stearns moved toward the boardwalk while Elliot's eyes followed the horse's progress down the street, his face slack-jawed and disbelieving. Stearns touched his arm and led him back into the saloon. Grabbing a bottle and a pair of glasses, he guided the sergeant upstairs to room number four.

The room was empty, the twin cots unruffled, and there was no sign of previous occupants. Stearns pushed Elliot on stumbling steps toward one of the cots, filled a glass to the brim and placed it in the sergeant's hand, then pulled the note from his pocket and stepped to the light of the window. The penmanship was crisp, clean and the note was almost a legal document for its precision.

Captain Stearns:

Corporal Culhane, the unresisting bearer of this note, met with unfortunate circumstances beyond his control. We take this somewhat disheartening means to inform you that we have fifteen thousand dollars in cash which we are willing to exchange for three hundred Spencer repeaters, which we know are in your possession. We would like to make arrangements for the transaction as quickly as possible. You will be contacted at our convenience. If our courier does not return with the proper response, one Corporal Thatcher will arrive in a similar condition to Corporal Culhane with a one-hundred-dollar bill affixed to his saber scabbard. That will mean we are no longer interested in dealing with you.

Yours,<br>THE DESERT SENTINELS

Sergeant Elliot was gaining control of his emotions now and he looked up with a surly snarl.

"What'd the dirty, miserable, good for nothing, murdering bastards have to say?"

Stearns tapped his chin with the note, deep in thought. "They know."

"Know what?"

"About the rifles."

"Who are they?"

Stearns looked at the scrap of paper again. "The Desert Sentinels."

"The who?"

The captain poured a drink, trying to collect his thoughts and make some sense of what he had just read.

"They have the money. They want the rifles. They have Thatcher and will kill him, which I don't give a damn about, if we don't do as they say quickly. Damnit!" Stearns said, slamming his fist on the table. "If we just had some time. Bibby will be gone in two days, but I know they won't wait that long. With him out of the way, I could work something out."

Stearns ran a hand through his hair in frustration. "The

rifles can't get stolen again, for God's sake! And we can't kill Bibby. We need some time!"

"Time we ain't got, Jason. Word of what happened to Wayne is gonna get back to that fort quicker'n ants to a picnic."

"Yeah, I know. When we get back there I'll restrict the entire brigade to quarters. And make the fort off limits to civilians. Nobody in or out except you and me. I'll make up some excuse to give to Bibby. That should keep Wayne's death a secret, at least on our end. Come on, let's go. We can't let anyone get out there before we do."

The two cavalry mounts were but twin streaks of dust to the sentry. He studied them until they came close enough for him to recognize Captain Stearns and Sergeant Elliot. Leaning over the parapet, he called down to the two soldiers lounging beside the gates. "Better throw open them doors, boys! Mean and meaner are headed this way, and them ain't smiles I see on their faces!"

The gates swung open and the two lathered horses pounded inside and slid to a halt. Captain Stearns leaped down and turned to Sergeant Elliot who was easing from the saddle.

"Assemble the troop, Sergeant! Every man, front and center, on the double!"

Colonel Bibby peeked out the window, alarmed at the captain's anger, but glad to see him striding toward his own quarters. Bibby quickly began stripping off his dress uniform and scrambling into his service blues.

Sergeant Elliot ran to the barracks and stood full silhouette in the doorway. "All right, you scum! I want every damned one of you front and center in one minute! Any man that's late'll be wearin' my knuckles for a grin!"

He whirled and went to the stable, the mess hall, the quartermaster supply and finally stopped to stare up at the sentry. "You stay up there, but listen up real good, hear me? What the cap'n's gonna say, you'd better hear."

The troops scrambled into formation and snapped to attention. Stearns stepped from his quarters with a long, black riding crop in his hands. He moved before the assembled soldiers like a panther on the prowl before turning and facing them in cold silence for nearly two minutes.

"You men are all restricted to quarters until further notice. Is that understood? To quarters, not just to the fort. Do your job, get it done, and return to the barracks."

The cooks and quartermaster corps, unused to standard military regimen, stood in a makeshift formation off to one side. Stearns approached them with menacing strides. "And that goes for you people as well! If you need something from town, ask me or Sergeant Elliot."

He went before the main assembly again. "There will be no civilians allowed on the premises for any reason. There will be no talking to civilians except to tell them they cannot gain entrance. If you are on sentry duty, ask that person to state his business and then report to me or the sergeant. Is that understood?"

Mumbles of agreement came from the ranks and one young private, either too stupid or innocent to know better, raised his hand. "Pardon me, sir, but why are we being confined to quarters?"

Stearns fell upon him like the wrath of God. "You, soldier! Front and center!"

The young man moved forward and stood before his captain. "Yes, sir?"

"You will not speak unless spoken to. If you do so, you, or the next man who disobeys an order, will receive five lashes from this quirt to be delivered upon the broad of the back by Sergeant Elliot. Now, fall in!"

The young soldier scurried back to his position and snapped to attention.

Captain Stearns paced before them again, stopped and gently tapped the riding crop against his thigh.

"Two of my men went AWOL last night. Trusted men. Corporal Thatcher and Corporal Culhane. Somewhere between here and the battle they broke ranks. They were seen by a rancher heading north early this morning. And I, a captain in the United States Cavalry, have to suffer the embarrassment of having that told to me by a civilian!

"We had a hard battle last night, and I wanted to let you men rest, so I called no formations today. And how am I thanked? Two men are missing. I will not tolerate disobedience. If any one of you so much as peeks a nose out that gate, or speaks to a civilian, I will have you whipped and thrown in the stockade for the remainder of your tour of duty here."

Stearns spun abruptly and stalked away in the direction of Colonel Bibby's office. "Sergeant Elliot," he called over his shoulder, "leave them stand in the sun for an hour, then dismiss them."

Bibby ducked away from the window again and assumed a nonchalant position behind his desk. When he heard the captain's boots on the steps, he began scribbling furiously on a pad opened before him. He was about to call for the captain to enter when Stearns stalked into the room. Bibby saw the look on the captain's face and wondered briefly what in hell had happened to those wonderful troops he had so diligently trained but who were now standing at attention under the boiling sun.

"Hello, Captain," he offered cautiously. "Won't you have a seat?"

Stearns ignored the question and turned to the orderly standing beside the door. "Corporal! Go to my quarters, double time! There's something on my table for the colonel. You'll know what it is. Bring it here immediately."

The alarm increased on Bibby's face and he wondered if the corporal might be bringing back a hatchet. "May I . . . may I offer you a drink, Captain?"

"No, you can't," Stearns said curtly, moving toward the window and looking out. "Goddamn them," he muttered. He saw the orderly running toward them now and added, "You'd better hustle your butt, soldier."

Stearns moved toward the door, took a bag from his hands

and slammed the door. Bibby had crossed to the far corner of the room and stood with his arms trembling by his sides, afraid even to assume his cocked stance.

Stearns dug in the bag and Bibby flinched as a hand flashed out. The captain examined a quart bottle before extending it toward the colonel with an amicable grin.

"This is for you, Colonel. Best whiskey available. I thought we might toast the purchase of your ticket?"

Bibby felt the blood flow through his legs again and took a testing step. "For me, Captain?"

"Certainly, for you," Stearns replied, jerking the cork out with a flourish. "The best damned commander this fort ever had shouldn't have to drink second-rate whiskey, now should he?"

Relief gushed from Bibby's chest in a great wheeze. The knuckles crept up to his spine and he was a whole man again. "No, by God. I guess not. Mighty decent of you, Captain. Mighty damned decent way for a junior officer . . . I mean for a captain to treat a colonel. What on your pay and all. Maybe when I get to Washington I can correct that oversight."

Grinning broadly, Stearns handed a glass over, touched the rim of his glass to Bibby's and drank. "Never hurts to have good friends in high places, Colonel."

Bibby sipped the whiskey and savored the mellow flavor. "God but that tastes wonderful. Haven't had whiskey like that since I left civilization."

"Ah, but you're going back to it now, right, sir? Here's to the good life."

Bibby matched the hefting of Stearns' glass and glanced cautiously toward the window.

"Ahhhem. If you don't mind my asking, Captain, I couldn't help noticing you weren't too pleased with the troops. Is there something wrong?"

Stearns brushed the thought away with a wave of his hand and a laugh. "Think nothing of it, Colonel. Just a little overdue discipline. You can't be expected to do everything around here. Two men went over the hill last night, that's all. We'll catch up with them in time. That's how I train my troops, Colonel. Make them police their own ranks. When Thatcher and Culhane are caught, those men standing out there in the sun will punish them far worse than I ever could. And, the next man who thinks of breaking ranks will give it a second thought before he goes."

"As a disciplinarian myself, I commend your approach," Bibby said, his mind totally away from the troops and onto a more important topic. "The telegram and my reservations have all been attended to, I take it?"

"Covered. You're as good as on your way to San Francisco right now." Stearns rose and placed an arm around Bibby's flabby shoulders. "Come, let's have another drink. This fort, and all the misery that goes with it, is no longer your concern. From this moment forth, what do you say if I attend to all matters of responsibility? That way, if I have any problems during the transition, I'll have you to help me out."

Bibby beamed his approval. "A princely idea, Captain." He squeezed his eyes together and his cheeks rose on his face. "Or, may I call you Commander?"

## Chapter Fifteen

It started as a faint tattoo and rapidly increased to a steady rumble as the pounding of hooves drew near. Rodrigo leaned forward from the wall and listened intently.

"One horse. That will be Juan."

Munn eased to the mouth of the arroyo and leveled his Colt at the entranceway. A dusty, weary horse plunged to a stop and the lithe Mexican jumped lightly from the saddle. He tapped Munn gently on a rock-hard stomach with his fist, grinned and ran to stand before Rodrigo. His eyes were bright and clear as he rattled off rapid-fire Spanish. He gesticulated with his hands, threw his head back and laughed, then continued talking for nearly another minute.

Blake listened to the tumble of words, but the only thing he could understand was *agua*, which he knew meant water in Spanish.

Rodrigo nodded, and when the young man fell silent, the Argentinian clapped his shoulders. "That is very good, Juan. Thank you. Now, eat and rest."

"It worked perfectly," Rodrigo said, turning toward Blake and Hank. "Juan went into the hills above town and waited until this afternoon when he saw Burke and Wyler going in to meet with Wayne and Tully. After he knew they had arrived, he set the horse free. Having not drunk since yesterday, he knew the horse would go to the nearest water, the troughs on the main street. Then he circled back and rode into town from the opposite direction. He doesn't speak any English, but he reads facial expressions well in any language. That's why he laughed when he told of the look on Burke's face. Fear is the word which would best describe it."

"Then they have your message and know we have the money?" Blake asked, feeling a growing excitement.

"Yes, they have our message. Both expressed and implied."

"What do we do now, Rod?"

"We send Sebastian to the fort. He speaks English very well, but he too will have a note. He will arrive there at ten o'clock tomorrow morning and ask to speak to Captain Stearns and Stearns only. He will hand the second note to him personally."

"Isn't that kind of like throwin' old Sebastian into a snake pit, Rod?" Hank asked. "He'll never get out of there alive."

"Yes he will," Rodrigo said with a firm smile. "If I thought differently, I wouldn't send him."

Fort Hastings resembled a buttoned-up shoe cast upon the desert. The gates were closed, there was no activity, and someone had even forgotten to put up the flag that morning. A single horse approached the somber wooden giant. A long dry pole was resting on a stirrup and a white piece of cloth hung limply in the absence of wind. The sentry lowered his rifle and Sebastian stopped twenty yards from the main gates.

"Hold it right there, Mexer! Name your business!"

Sebastian smiled with eternal patience and innocence in a way that only the Spanish can duplicate.

"Pleeeese berry much, señor. I hab soomthing for captain."

The soldier scowled down. Is a Mexican a civilian? he asked himself. Taking no chances on definitions, he leaned over and yelled to the soldier waiting below. "There's a Mexer out here that wants to speak to the captain. He's here under a flag of truce for some damned reason. What do I tell him?"

"Tell him to hold onto his tortillas. I'll see if the captain is in a talking mood."

"Glad it's you and not me," the soldier above said with obvious relief before turning to scowl down at Sebastian again.

## The Desert Sentinels

Davis knocked gently on the captain's door. "Captain Stearns, sir? There's somebody here to see you."

A long pause, a bed squeaked, then the door snapped open. "Yes, Davis? What is it?"

"Sorry to bother you, sir, but there's a Mexican at the gate and he wants to talk with you."

"Are you crazy, man? I haven't got time for Mexicans, and I told you I didn't want anyone . . ."

"He's carrying a white flag, sir."

"A what?"

"A white flag, sir. I wouldn't have bothered you if . . ."

Stearns brushed past him, crossing the parade ground with long, menacing strides. "Open one gate!"

The gate opened just wide enough for a man's body and Stearns stepped through.

"Sentry! I want your rifle aimed at this man's chest at all times," Stearns said, his eyes never leaving Sebastian's face.

"Yes, sir!"

Sebastian smiled pleasantly. "*Buenos dias*, soor."

"Get off that horse. I look up to no man when I speak."

Continuing to smile, Sebastian stepped down.

"Why are you here?"

"I have note for jew."

"From whom?"

"El Sentinels of the—how you say—desert?" Sebastian grinned at the grimace tightening Captain Stearns' face. But he offered no note.

"Okay, goddamnit! Where's the note?"

Sebastian fumbled in his pocket, enjoying Stearns' anger and playing it to the limit. Finally he found a folded square of paper in his hip pocket. "Berry sorry, soor. Berry sorry," he said, handing the note over. "Me jus poor *el stupido* Mexican."

"Damned right you are," Stearns growled, snatching the note and turning toward the gate.

"*Un momento, por favor.* Ah, excuse please. El Sen*'* They want answer."

Stearns watched Sebastian warily, glanced at the sentry to make sure of his position, then read the note.

Captain Stearns:

Corporal Thatcher was not quite ready yet, so we had to send Sebastian with this communique. You and Elliot are to meet with me and a companion at the saloon in Twin Buttes at exactly two o'clock this afternoon. Do not bother bringing reinforcements or planning any treachery. If ill-fate befalls us, your fifteen thousand will be gone. And that holds true for Sebastian as well. If he does not return safely, our deal is off.

Stearns folded the note and stuck it into his pocket. "Tell them we'll be there."

Sebastian looked confused. "Berry slow, Captain. Please, berry slow."

Frustrated, Stearns placed his hands on his hips and shouted into the Mexican's face. "Tell-them-we-will-be-there!"

Sebastian scrubbed his ears and grinned. "*Gracias*, Captain. Berry slow, good. Berry loud, not good. Maybe you write for me." He shrugged with that infuriatingly patient smile. "Excuse poor *el dumbo* Mexicano. No educate like Americano captain." He pulled the stub of a pencil from his shirt pocket and offered it to the captain.

Stearns swore under his breath, leaned against the wall and wrote his reply on the back of the message before thrusting it impatiently at Sebastian. "Here! And you're goddamned right, you are a stupid, ignorant Mexican. One day you and your people will feel the bite of American steel! Now get the hell out of here."

Sebastian swung up and the grin faded into hard bitterness. "And you, Captain, are a liar, a murderer, a thief and a fool. You couldn't hold an honest Mexican's hat, which most of us are. And I long for the day when I can meet you on the battlefield."

Sebastian spat upon the ground, pulled the horse's head up and galloped into the desert.

Stearns watched him leave, slack-jawed. The perfectly spoken English rang in his ears and he could feel the mocking eyes of the sentry on his back. He whirled and leveled a stiff finger at the grinning soldier.

"You! Wipe that look off your face or I'll bust it off. Four hours extra duty tonight! And, if one word of what has happened out here comes back to me, you'll feel the lash until your bones are raw!"

Stearns stalked through the gate and the wooden section closed behind, sealing off the fort again. When the captain was safely in his quarters, the sentry turned toward the desert and laughed silently until the tears ran down his cheeks. Then he wiped his eyes and watched a buckboard approach from the direction of town. An elderly, pot-bellied man sat in the seat and steadily drew nearer the gate.

"Oh, no," the sentry groaned. "Not again."

The buckboard stopped and the driver stared at the gates questioningly before looking up at the sentry.

"Good morning. I'm Luther Masters and I'd like to talk with Captain Stearns."

"Good morning, sir. I'm sorry, but there's no way me or anybody else is going to bother the captain now."

"What do you mean, bother him? This is business. I am an agent for the stage line and I have a voucher here that is due and payable to me. My daughter was assured by the captain that he would take care of it personally."

"I'm sorry, sir. Come back another time."

"Come back another time, hell! That's a long ride, soldier. Of course you wouldn't know, you fellows never come into town anymore. There isn't a business in Twin Buttes that doesn't depend on your trade. What the hell's going on out here?"

The sentry glanced first toward the captain's quarters t

down at the merchant. "We can't come to town," he said, his voice just above a whisper. "We're restricted to quarters."

"Why?"

"Can't talk no more, sir. Captain's orders."

Luther Masters fought a mental battle between puzzlement and anger. Anger was the victor. "Well, you tell your high and mighty captain that I run a cash only business! He might run this fort, but he damned well doesn't run our town!"

"You tell him that, sir, when you see him. I ain't tellin' him nothin'. Good day, sir."

"Good day to you, soldier!" Masters snapped, cracking the whip over his bay mare. "And when you fellows want a little credit in the future, just remember our little conversation today!"

The sentry shook his head sadly and watched the buckboard churn away in a swirl of dust. "Damn," he mumbled. Credit was his life's blood.

## Chapter Sixteen

The sun, at two o'clock in the afternoon, had nearly reduced Twin Buttes to a ghost town. Few horses were at the hitching rails and the townspeople were laid up inside seeking whatever coolness they could find.

Captain Stearns' shirt was damp across the shoulders and down his spine while Sergeant Elliot's clung to him like a damp mop. With eyes sweeping the street on all sides, they rode cautiously toward the saloon and were now abreast of the stage office.

Gloria Masters glanced toward the window, gasped in surprise, touched her hair, and pulling her skirts aside, she rushed to the door.

"Captain Stearns? Oh, Captain Stearns?"

Stearns pulled his horse up and looked back with irritation obvious on his face. "Not now, Miss Masters," he said curtly.

Her step faltered and a hurt look filled her eyes. "I only wanted to tell you . . ."

"Not now. I'm busy. Talk to me later."

"But, Father . . ."

"I don't give a damn about your father!" Stearns snarled, jerking the horse's head around and angling toward the saloon.

Gloria Masters watched the two men dismount and glance once through the window before moving quickly inside. The hurt in her eyes became anger, and she swished her skirts in helpless disgust before returning to the stage office with huffy strides.

Ten minutes later, another pair of horses passed along the

main street and their riders were equally cautious and wary.

"Looks pretty deserted, Rod," Blake offered.

"That's why I chose this time of day." Rodrigo nodded toward the two cavalry mounts. "They're here."

"Good. I've waited for this moment a long time."

They stepped down before the hitching rail and looped their reins over the pole, then Blake stood beside the door while Rodrigo glanced through the window. The saloon was empty except for the bartender, who stood at the far end of the bar reading a newspaper, and two soldiers seated at a table against the back wall and facing the door. They stepped inside and stood apart, hands resting a fraction of an inch from the butt of their Colts.

Blake's eyes searched out Luke Wyler's face, and the crushing hatred closed over his mind.

Surprise registered on Wyler's face, but it quickly became a contemptuous sneer. His voice boomed in the stillness. "Well, if it ain't Blake Evans, the man who killed his own brother." The eyes narrowed to furrowed slits. "And mine!"

Blake's hand quivered over his gun and the calmness in Rodrigo's voice was all that stopped him from smashing the life from the man before him.

"Hold on, Blake. We're in this together. Your time will come."

The tension eased in Blake's upper body and he fell in step with the Argentinian. Rodrigo pulled out two chairs, turned them backwards and shoved one toward Blake before sitting down with his arms on the back rest and his Colt hanging free on one side.

"Are you the so-called Desert Sentinels?" Stearns asked, his voice icy like his face.

"That we are. Some of them," Rodrigo replied cordially. "But, two things before we talk. The guns first. You and Wyler take those revolvers from your laps and lay them on the table. Blake and I will do the same. Then, we'll have a drink. Agreed?"

There was a momentary pause, then all four weapons

moved to the center of the table simultaneously. Rodrigo smiled his satisfaction, and he spoke without taking his eyes off Stearns.

"Bartender?"

"Yes?" the old man answered, his voice weak.

"Bring us a bottle and four glasses. Serve them on a tray, if you have one."

"Yes, sir," the bartender replied, quickly filling the order and crossing to the table. "Will there be anything else?"

"One more thing. Put those weapons on your tray and leave them at the bar. Then, please step into the back room, close the door and wait there until we've finished with our conversation."

The old man picked up the guns, dropped the tray onto the bar, then scurried into the storage room and the door closed behind him with a solid thud.

Stearns smiled coldly. "Are you through playing games?"

"Games?" Rodrigo asked. "Since when is murder a game?"

"Culhane didn't exactly come in here telling jokes."

"He was murdered by you two bastards, that's what!" Big Luke raged, his moustache quivering.

"Wrong. He killed himself. But that's neither here nor there."

"Culhane, huh, Luke?" Blake asked in mock surprise. "Are you and Frank so ashamed of your family name that you had it changed? If so, I can understand it. Folks up in Fargo, Dakota Territory, still think you're the leader of the Wyler gang. Gonna be real disappointed when they find out the leader of the Culhane gang died in Arizona."

"Who's gonna kill me, Blake? A worthless sodbuster like you?"

"Another member of your gang felt the same way. He died in Fargo."

Luke Wyler remembered Will's speed with a gun, and a grudging respect came into his eyes. "He mighta had a little difficulty killin' his own brother. Apparently you didn't."

"No more than I'm going to have killing you."

Somehow, the deadly tone in Blake's voice startled Wyler and he downed his whiskey without reply.

"You know, Captain, I have to congratulate you," Rodrigo began, filling the glasses again. "Your Corporal Thatcher is a hell of a man. You must be a real leader. I've tried a few persuasive tricks on him, and short of killing him, I don't know what to do. He won't talk, won't tell me a damned thing. Like I said, he's a helluva man."

"He's still alive then?"

"Very much so."

"I want him back."

"And you can have him. When the exchange is made."

"And when will that be?"

"That's what we're here to discuss, isn't it?"

"Get to the point, damnit!"

"In due time, Captain, in due time. What is the condition of the rifles?"

"Excellent."

Rodrigo shook his head in surprise. "Even after they've changed hands so many times? Must be durable weapons."

"They are. And the fifteen thousand?"

"Dry and crisp. As you'll see tomorrow."

Stearns edged forward slightly. He remembered Bibby's departure on the morning stage and he saw hope. "When, tomorrow?"

"At twelve o'clock noon."

"Where?"

"Are you familiar with Little Poison Lake? Perfect place for an ambush."

"It is and I am."

"That's precisely why we won't be making the exchange there."

"Then where? Get on with it man, for God's sake!"

The easy smile was on Rodrigo's face again. "Such haste, Captain. Such haste. You and your swine mascot there are in good company for the first time in your lives, and you want to leave so quickly?"

## The Desert Sentinels

Big Luke bristled and Stearns touched his arm. "Later, Luke. He's holding the aces right now. But he won't always have them. Where?"

"There is a promontory just south of Little Poison. The desert is flat for miles around. We will meet halfway between the promontory and the lake at noon tomorrow. Yourself, Wyler here," he paused to glance at Big Luke. "Or do you prefer Sergeant Elliot?"

"You go to hell!"

Rodrigo shrugged and continued. "This ignoramus, by whatever name, his brother and Private Davidson will meet with Blake, Hank Lane, Biggie Munn and myself. One of my men will be posted on the promontory. If he sees any of your forces close enough to attack, he'll fire a warning shot and we'll be gone to Mexico with your fifteen thousand dollars. There will be the four of us against the four of you. We'll have the money, and you'll have the rifles. And, if you can control your treachery long enough, we'll part, each having what he came for."

A plan was already whirling through Stearns' brain but he kept his face calm and his voice even. "Fair enough."

"How we gonna get the rifles out of the fort in broad daylight, Cap'n?" Big Luke asked.

"That's an interesting question, Captain Stearns," Rodrigo added. "How will you manage that?"

"None of your damned business. I'll work it out. You just be there with the money."

"Well said, but, if I may correct you, it is my business. Those are my rifles."

"Not just yet they aren't. When I have the money in my hands, then they'll be your rifles. However temporary that condition might be. Is that all?"

Rodrigo nodded. "As far as I'm concerned it is, but I think my friend has some business to conduct with your baboon."

Blake watched Luke Wyler and the hatred gnawed at the corners of his mind. Across from him sat the man responsible for the deaths of his parents and ruination of his brother. And yet he could not touch him. He would have to carry the hatred for another day before the pent-up vengeance, years in the building, could be spent with blinding, cleansing fury. Blake pushed his glass away and leaned back. "Tomorrow, Luke, after the exchange, you and I are going into the desert alone. Only one of us will be coming back."

Big Luke guffawed and filled his glass again. "That's right fine with me, Blake. I don't mind ridin' both ways."

Captain Stearns placed his hands on the table and pushed the chair back with his legs. "If you gentlemen will excuse me, I have some important business to conduct."

All four men stood and faced each other across the small table. "Yes, I'd say you have," Rodrigo replied while turning his head slightly toward the store room and raising his voice. "Bartender! Please come in here."

"Yes, sir!" the old man answered, pushing the door open slowly and peering around before stepping into the room.

"Bring that tray over here and place it in the center of the table. Then move back out of the way."

"Yes, sir," the bartender said, snatching the tray, dropping it onto the table and darting behind the bar.

Rodrigo stood with his hands by his sides and watched the captain's face. "Go for your gun, Stearns," he said without emotion. "Whoever comes up last pays for the whiskey."

Stearns hesitated, glancing from Rodrigo's face to the tray of weapons then back to the cold, brown mask. The corner of his mouth twitched and his fingers quivered. Then his hand flashed to the tray, and snatching the service revolver nearest to him, he leveled the weapon. He was looking down the barrel of a Colt Forty-four. Rodrigo's finger teased the trigger before he lowered the hammer.

"Looks like you pay, Captain. And don't forget to tip the bartender for his kindness."

Stearns jammed the revolver into its holster before digging some coins from his pocket which he threw onto the table. His face was beet red and twisted in rage.

"Get your weapon, Sergeant, and let's go."

"Get your weapon, Sergeant," Blake mocked. "You always needed someone to do your thinking for you in life, Luke. Looks like you've finally found your calling. A phoney captain's lackey."

The baiting words seared Big Luke's ears and his body trembled with the desire to kill.

"You'll get yours, Evans," he blurted, holstering the revolver. "Tomorrow, you'll get yours! And, I'm gonna kill you slow and love every minute of watching you die."

Blake smiled easily as he watched the two uniformed men move toward the door. "Don't forget to let the captain go ahead of you, Luke. Remember your place in life."

Big Luke surged ahead of the captain and slammed his way through the batwing doors.

## Chapter Seventeen

An evening hush had settled over the fort, but the heat of day had not yet yielded to the cooling air of night. The troops filled the square beneath the flag pole, standing at parade rest in tight rows that might have been a field of yellow and blue corn.

Lieutenant Ashford was proud of his soldiers. He had drilled them mercilessly throughout the afternoon, upon Captain Stearns' orders, and now, weary though they were, they stood tall like a unit of first-rank cavalry troopers. He saw the wagon enter the main gateway, with Sergeant Elliot on the seat and Captain Stearns riding just ahead and leading the sergeant's mount, and his chest swelled against the salt-streaked cloth around his upper body. He wondered what the captain was doing with a rented civilian wagon, but he knew better than to ask, and when the captain stepped down, Ashford squared away before the company.

"Company! Tennnnnshut!"

Sabers rattled and leather heels clicked together in unison. Captain Stearns looked at the soldiers and allowed a pleasant smile to soften his drawn face. "Very good, Lieutenant. Very good indeed," he said, wandering up and down the ranks. Not a man looked right or left. Rifles were held stiffly placed against right legs, and left hands, fingers extended full length, pointed directly at the dusty earth.

Stearns was standing beside the ramrod-stiff lieutenant again now. "I am truly impressed, Mr. Ashford. Put the troops at ease."

"At heeeese!"

Another rattle, the motion of feet.

"I know you men have been drilled hard today," Stearns began with evident satisfaction, "and I'm proud of the accomplishments you have made. You're beginning to look like a fighting unit now, and I think you deserve a little reward. While you're still restricted to the fort for the time being, there is no reason why we can't have some fun amongst ourselves. Sergeant Elliot? Would you bring the wagon forward, please?"

Reins clicked and the team moved to a position in front of the ranks. Stearns nodded and waved a hand. "Go ahead, Sergeant, show the men what the rewards are for hard work and diligence."

Elliot stooped and grasped a crate which he raised high above his head. There was a uniform gasp of surprise as the troops stared at the crate brandished to the sky above thickly muscled arms. One soldier mustered up enough courage to ask what was on everyone's mind.

"Is that whiskey, sir?"

"Yes it is, Private. Three cases of whiskey and two barrels of beer. Now, as you know, tomorrow is Colonel Bibby's last day as your commanding officer. Tonight, we're going to have the biggest party this territory has ever seen."

Throaty, dry cheers echoed across the abandoned desert. Stearns smiled indulgently while holding his hands up for silence.

"Okay, men, listen up now. I'm going to have the cooks prepare a buffet and it will be open mess for those of you who want to eat. For those of you who don't, the booze is yours as quickly as you can get to your barracks. Tennnshut!"

The troops snapped to immediate statuesque positions and held. Stearns saluted them then turned to the lieutenant.

"Lieutenant Ashford, you select a detachment of twenty men for any possible patrols that might be necessary. They'll get theirs tomorrow, but tonight we need some troops capable of sitting a saddle. You will be in charge of that detachment, and tomorrow afternoon you and they will be given passes into town with government vouchers for your expenses. Send Private Moody and Private Davidson to my quarters after you've dismissed the troop, and you can dismiss them now, if you wish."

They matched crisp salutes and Stearns turned toward his quarters. He heard a loud, "'A' troop! Stay in formation! Private Moody and Private Davidson, the captain wants to see you in his quarters! The remainder of the company . . . dissssmisssed!" and the following hoots and yells and pounding of boots on the parade grounds. Stearns smiled and stepped into his quarters.

After pouring a glass of whiskey for each of the men in the room, Stearns passed them around then cocked a foot on his bunk.

"Luke and I met with these Desert Sentinels today. One of them is the bastard we almost hung, and the other is the Mexican who took me hostage. They say they are willing to trade the fifteen thousand for the rifles." He looked directly at Frank Wyler. "They also killed your brother, Frank."

Shock registered on Frank Wyler's face and his eyes drifted slowly from Burke's face to Big Luke's. "That true, Luke?"

"True. Tortured him till he was dead, then sent him into town tied to his saddle. Blake Evans is one of them Desert . . . whatever they call themselves. An' he's gonna be a dead man tomorrow."

"Blake? What the hell's he doin' here?"

"Beats me. But he's here. Sorry about Wayne, Frank."

"What the hell can you say?"

"Nothin'. But we can do. And do we will tomorrow."

"Luke and I have it figured where we'll get the money back, keep the rifles and leave them dead in the desert," Stearns said, pulling a map from the shelf and spreading it across the cot. He stabbed a finger at the location assigned by Rodrigo for the rendezvous. "We meet there at twelve o'clock noon tomorrow. With the rifles."

Moody squinted at the map before taking in the captain. "How we gonna get the rifles out of the fort, Cap'n? 'Cause if we can, they've picked the perfect place for an ambush. There's a canyon deep enough to hide a troop of cavalry runnin' parallel to that spot and not a quarter of a mile away."

"I know it, Moody. We'll get the rifles out tonight. That's what the whiskey's for. Everybody in this fort will be so drunk by midnight that we could steal the walls and nobody'd know it. We'll load the wagon at two o'clock this morning and meet them there by noon."

Frank looked at the map and shook his head. "Just the four of us against them? How many men have they got? Maybe they've got a little ambush brewin' in their own stewpot."

"There won't be just the four of us. Lieutenant Ashford doesn't know it yet, but by noon tomorrow, he'll be a hero. His detachment will be in that draw, and we'll have a little surprise in the wagon the Sentinels aren't counting on. When Ashford hears the firing, he'll come at a gallop. We'll have twenty-eight men against their four."

Big Luke refilled his glass. "How 'bout Bibby, Jason? He's gotta be on that stage tomorrow mornin'. Didn't you say he was countin' on you kissin' him good-bye?"

"I'm going to take care of that right now," Burke replied, taking two quarts of whiskey from the shelf. "He'll be so hung over in the morning he won't know if he's afoot or on horseback. Corporal Darby can make sure he doesn't miss that stage." He stepped toward the door. "Tomorrow it will be all over, gentlemen. We'll have the fifteen thousand, the rifles and control of the fort. Then we'll go to work on those silver shipments. From here on, it's all gravy. Stay sober, be at the quartermaster supply at two o'clock in the morning. And, bring four troopers armed to the teeth with you."

Rodrigo chewed the dried beef methodically and thought about Hank's question.

"You're right, Hank. There probably will be an ambush set up somewhere along the line. I hope it will be in the most obvious place, which is near where we will meet with Burke and

Wyler. I chose that location in the hope of lulling them into a false sense of security."

"What good is that going to do us, Rod?" Hank asked, not satisfied with the answer. "If he's got a unit of cavalry in that canyon, our sentries won't be able to see them and they'll be on us before we can get two miles in the direction of Mexico."

Rodrigo smiled. "That's fine. Because, we won't be going to Mexico."

"What? Then where the hell are we going with three hundred rifles?"

"Back to Fort Hastings."

"That's grand! Hand me that wineskin, Blake, old pal. I'd rather hang drunk than sober."

Blake handed the skin across while watching Rodrigo closely. "You didn't explain that too damned good, Rod. I'm afraid I'm with Hank. Why in hell would we be going back to the fort?"

Rodrigo glanced at Munn who stood nearby. "Munn? Would you mind getting Tully and bringing him here for me?"

Biggie Munn went to the rear of the arroyo and reappeared moments later with the prisoner. Tully walked free of shackles and bindings, looking well fed and rested.

"You wanted to see me?" he asked Rodrigo.

"Yes, Tully. Sit down here, roll yourself a smoke and help yourself to some wine."

Tully fashioned a cigarette, touched it with flame, squirted a long draught of wine over stained, rotting teeth and settled back to learn of his fate.

"Okay. What's on your mind?"

"We've treated you pretty well, haven't we, Orville?"

"Yup, I'll allow as to how ya have. Better'n I woulda treated you, as a matter of fact."

"I don't doubt that. Tell me, what was to be your percentage of the fifteen thousand?"

"A little less than three thousand."

"And with Wayne dead?"

"Closer to four. What difference does it make? We both know I'll never be leavin' here alive."

"I'll explain that in good time. How would you like to have your four thousand, a discharge from the army and your total freedom?"

"Like I'd like a big blonde, a quart of whiskey and the fastest horse in the territory. But how the hell am I gonna get it?"

"Colonel Bibby will give it to you."

Everyone in the arroyo who could speak English looked at Rodrigo as though he had gone mad, with the exception of Munn whose face remained impassive.

"Orville, give me a shot of that wine," Hank said. "Obviously I ain't listenin' too good sober."

"Could you explain that, Rod?" Blake asked.

"Of course. As soon as Mr. Tully is convinced. When he is, I'll explain it to you and then him in the morning. If he does his job properly, he will get four thousand dollars, his release from the service and his freedom to go wherever he pleases. If he does not, he will be dead and, therefore, not needing of four thousand dollars. What will it be, Orville?"

"Don't look like they's a helluva lot of decisions to be made here, pardner. Tell me what to do, and I give you my word, if I can do it, it'll get done."

"Your word, huh, Orville," Hank said with a derisive laugh. "That's kind of like givin' a rattlesnake first bite, ain't it?"

Tully's eyes became cold and deadly. "When a man from Virginny gives his word, you'd better hope it ain't a price on your head, that's all I gotta say. I may be a little adrift in some respects, but I still got pride in my word."

"Especially when it's worth four thousand bucks, which I know damned well it ain't."

"That's enough, Hank," Rodrigo broke in. "I believe Orville is a man of his word. He's got guts, and he's a fighter. I'll accept your word, Mr. Tully. Do I have it?"

"It's yours."

"Fine. You've just earned your life and a few dollars

change. Maybe even a little touch of self-respect. Now, if you'll kindly go back to your quarters, I have some things to discuss with the others. Get some rest. We leave at first light in the morning."

Colonel Bibby blinked and tried to focus on the blurred image swimming before his eyes. He raised the glass and caught half his mouth and was mindless of the whiskey dripping onto his chest.

"You're a good man, Cap'n Stea . . . Sark . . . ah . . . Captain. Haven't had a party like this since the war got over." He blinked again. "The war is over, isn't it?" he asked as his head drifted toward his chest.

Captain Stearns watched him like a mother might, hovering over her child and lulling it to sleep with soft, comforting words.

"The war is over for you, Colonel. Tomorrow you will be on that stage, rocking softly in the seat, gently rocking, ever drawing nearer San Francisco. The coach sways gently on its hinges and Colonel Nevis Bibby relaxes on the seat in the warm sunlight, knowing he's done a good job, and sleeps soundly in the knowledge that he is going back to civilization. The stage rocks gently and Colonel Bibby's eyes get heavy and he sleeps peacefully. Peacefully, ever so peacefully."

Bibby's head lolled to one side, his eyes fluttered once, his mouth fell open and his head slowly dropped to crossed arms on the desk top.

Captain Stearns sat motionless, waiting for the whiskey to completely seal off the colonel's mind. He glanced at the tall clock standing against the wall. One-thirty. He listened for sounds coming from the barracks and heard none. And he knew Lieutenant Ashford and his detachment would be sleeping soundly in preparation for the morning's patrol, after having been relieved at midnight watch by Sergeant Elliot, Private Moody and Private Davidson. He rose and moved cautiously toward the door on tiptoes. The boards squeaked beneath his feet, but Bibby continued his soft snoring.

Once on the parade ground, Stearns raced across the square to the main gate and called up to Moody and Davidson. "Okay, let's go. We've got half an hour."

Elliot was leading the six-mule span to the quartermaster's building as they rounded the corner, and four soldiers, with their weapons beside them, were passed out in the back of the wagon.

They worked quickly, carrying the crates from the storage shed and placing them gently on the wagon bed before a canvas was stretched over the top and lashed down. Private Davidson climbed on the seat while Stearns, Moody and Elliot swung into their saddles, and leading a spare horse behind them, they passed through the gate just as the colonel's clock chimed two bells. Elliot paused to close the gates, then galloped to catch up with the others.

Rodrigo watched from halfway up the promontory and saw the wagon's dust trail from several miles away, moving across the flat, open desert and steadily toward them.

"Here they come," he said to Blake and handed the glasses across. "Looks like just the four of them."

"Yeah, it does," Blake agreed. "Think Tully will be able to pull it off?"

"He'd better. For our sake as well as his. Let's go, they'll be halfway by the time we get there."

Riding slowly onto the great expanse of white, Rodrigo, Hank, Blake and Biggie Munn moved toward the rising dust cloud four abreast with the packhorse trailing behind. As the two forces drew near, all eyes were searching the desert for the ambush each knew was expected.

Blake sought out the tall, thick-bodied man in the lead, and his pulse quickened with a surge of adrenalin. He recognized Frank Wyler now and wondered briefly which of the two brothers he hated the most. Then he noticed the tarpaulin with its lashings hanging loose from their tie downs.

"Watch the wagon, Rod," he whispered. "Canvas isn't tied down."

Rodrigo nodded and they pulled their horses to a stop twenty yards in front of the wagon. Hands rested near guns and eight pairs of hating, faithless eyes watched in consuming silence.

Corporal Hurlong rode along the sandy bottom of the shallow canyon beside Lieutenant Ashford and pushed his hat back to mop his brow.

"If you don't mind my sayin' so, Lieutenant, Captain Stearns has gotta be out of his cotton pickin' mind to have men and horses out in heat like this."

The lieutenant nodded and moisture glistened on his sparse moustache. "Our job is not to question the captain's orders, Hurlong, it is to follow them to the letter. We were supposed to be directly opposite the promontory at twelve o'clock noon by way of this canyon. We are on schedule, we'll be there in ten minutes like we're supposed to be, and that's all that matters. The captain told me I would know what to do when the time came and . . ."

Lieutenant Ashford jerked his horse in hard and his hand flashed palm outward above his shoulder. The eighteen riders behind him stopped on the signal and they all watched a cavalry mount plunge down the bank and wheel toward them. The trooper's uniform was torn, soiled and flapping from his shoulders as he urged his horse recklessly along the rocky bottom.

"Isn't that Corporal Thatcher, sir?" Hurlong asked, not believing his eyes.

The lieutenant squinted against the sun's glare. "Yes, I believe it is. Why would a deserter be coming toward us like he had hell in his hip pocket?" he asked, mostly to himself.

In that instant the faint rattle of staccato gunfire rolled over the canyon wall, and Ashford, fearful of ambush, glanced nervously toward the sound.

Thatcher pulled his plunging horse to a sliding stop and wiped his dry mouth with the back of a hand. "Mighty glad to see you, sir," he panted with a wide grin.

"Glad to see me, Corporal? Why would a deserter be glad to see an officer of the United States Cavalry?"

"Deserter?" Thatcher asked in total shock. "You got it all wrong, sir! Me and Culhane was taken prisoner by part of them Mexicans what was tryin' to steal the rifles. Culhane is dead, and I just now got away."

"How?"

Thatcher cocked an ear and listened to the increasing rifle fire. "Ain't got much time to talk, Lieutenant. Captain Stearns and his unit is pinned down beside the river right now and their position ain't much worth a damn. We gotta help 'em."

Ashford's head jerked toward the sound of firing again. "Pinned down? Where along the river?"

"At the crossing. They was jumped this mornin' and tried to make a run for it. They won't last long if we don't get there in a real sudden hurry. I snuck away when they went after the captain. I was on my way to the fort for help when I run into you."

Ashford hesitated, calculating, trying to make a decision. Thatcher urged his horse forward. "Lieutenant, we ain't got much time."

"How many are there?"

"A bunch."

Ashford listened again. "Those don't sound like Spencers to me."

Thatcher shook his head and his face became somber. "Might be we're too late already, sir."

The young lieutenant had heard enough. He spurred his horse and led the double column of plunging horses up the bank and toward the river.

The sound of firing was even fainter to Rodrigo's ears, but he heard it and knew the captain had as well. He watched the startled look in the captain's eyes and smiled, his eyes hard and cold. He saw a faint wisp of dust rising from back along the canyon and headed toward the river. He nodded in that direction.

"Turn around and look, Captain Stearns. Your men are chasing ghosts."

Stearns risked a glance, and when he saw the dust he could not conceal the grimace tightening his face.

"Who's at the river?"

"My men. They're shooting fish. When your detachment arrives, they will lead them a merry chase and give us time to complete our deal as gentlemen."

Stearns glanced nervously at Big Luke and his glance was met. The captain shrugged and looked at Rodrigo again.

"Have you got the money?"

"Do you have the rifles?"

"Yes. Would you like to inspect them?"

"Indeed."

With that word, Blake, Hank and Munn turned their mounts and fanned out, leaving fifteen yards between each of the four horses.

"Throw the tarp back, Frank," Wyler said with his hand inching across his waist.

Frank laid the reins on the floorboards and wiped sweaty palms against his thighs. He kicked the wagon seat twice, as if by accident, as he climbed down. His hand went to the canvas, and the tarpaulin bobbed once in the center as if a man were adjusting himself for a better position. The tarp whipped back and four soldiers lunged to their feet.

Munn and Rodrigo fired in the same instant and two soldiers toppled over the sideboard while Hank's shot took out a third. Frank Wyler pulled his revolver and was ducking behind a wheel when Blake's Colt exploded, sending a slug crashing through the side of Wyler's chest.

Big Luke's horse reared and Stearns' mount spun sideways. Private Moody fired before his rifle was to his shoulder and Hank's horse lunged upward before sagging to the ground with blood pouring from its neck. Then Moody whipped backward over his horse's rump, the victim of Rodrigo's second shot. The fourth soldier dropped his rifle to the floor of the wagon and held up his hands.

Stearns fired over his left arm as he spun his horse around and the bullet tore a searing gash along Blake's left cheek. Blake felt nothing. Luke Wyler spun around for a shot, and Blake's next bullet slammed into the hard leather cantle on Wyler's saddle. The horse staggered and Big Luke's shot went wild. Stearns fired again and Blake saw Munn's horse go down. His head snapped toward the gypsy, and he saw blood pouring from Munn's right shoulder before he disappeared beneath the tumbling horse.

Blake fired again and the bullet smashed into Stearns' left thigh. The captain looked down with a stunned, hurt look filling his eyes. The blue uniform quickly soaked up the blood and became a patch of crimson. Stearns whipped his horse's head around, and crouching low over its neck, he kicked the mount with his good leg and angled toward the canyon at a dead run. Before turning his horse, Big Luke fired one last shot at Blake but the bullet went wide, then he dug his spurs into the animal's flanks and raced after Stearns.

Blake and Hank fired in nearly the same instant and Blake thought he saw the big man flinch, but he remained low in the saddle and going away. Rodrigo leaped to the ground and threw his reins to Hank.

"Here, Hank! It's up to you and Blake. I'll take care of Munn."

Hank grinned. "Thanks, Rod. Me and Blake got some special debts to settle." He was on the horse's back and sinking the spurs home before the last word was said.

Their horses were neck and neck as Blake and Hank urged them after the two mounts now halfway to the lip of the canyon. Glancing toward the north, Blake saw the dust cloud again and knew the cavalry unit had gone to the river and was now heading toward the sound of battle at maximum speed. He pointed toward the dust cloud and yelled across, "We've got to get to Stearns before they get here! He'd lie his way out of this sure as hell!"

Hank nodded and raked the horse again with his spurs. Still out of rifle range, the two horses ahead plunged over the lip of the canyon. Blake and Hank worked their rifles free of saddle scabbards and braced for the careening lunge over and down. They slowed their mounts just short of the canyon's edge and the horses went down with forelegs braced in a lurching, bucking slide.

One horse lay on the sandy bottom with head raised and nostrils flared in pain. Its right front leg was twisted forward and up at a grotesque angle. Yards away, Big Luke was fighting desperately to get a foot in the stirrup of Stearns' horse and swing up behind the captain. Blake raised his rifle and fired quickly at Big Luke. It was a poorly aimed shot and the bullet thudded into the horse's haunch with a wicked slap. The horse sagged in a spin, trying to maintain balance before rearing over backwards.

Wyler scrambled away from the horse, fired two wild shots and limped toward a pile of boulders and debris. Captain Stearns fell heavily from the saddle, rolled over on his stomach and aimed his service revolver with both hands. Hank was off his horse now, aiming his rifle carefully before firing. The bullet crashed into the captain's right shoulder, tore through his chest and ripped a huge hole in the opposite side of his uniform just below the rib cage. Stearns' pistol dipped just as he squeezed the trigger and a cloud of sand exploded in a small geyser twenty feet in front of him. Then his head slumped forward and he lay motionless in the sand.

Moving to the shelter of the canyon wall, they saw a flash of blue in the rocks above and knew Wyler was trying to get into position. They crouched behind a boulder and Blake touched Hank's shoulder.

"He's mine, Hank. I'll take him alone."

"No, Blake. We'd better work together . . ."

"No, damnit! I want him for Ma and Pa."

Fire belched and a bullet smacked against the rock before singing a dying whine into the vast emptiness. Hank nodded and fired three quick shots while Blake reloaded his Colt. Then Blake dodged forward with the rifle held loosely in his grasp and clambered up the canyon wall to an outcropping of rock. Wyler's next shot tore the heel from Blake's boot as he dove into a sandstone crevasse. He raised up, fired once at where the last shot had come from, and ducked down again. He studied the terrain from around the edge of the outcropping and he knew Luke Wyler was trapped. And so was he. Blake brushed the sweat from his forehead and listened to the silence. Until the silence was broken.

Coiled, tongue licking, buzzing now, louder and louder, head raising and tail whipping, the rattlesnake was lying not five feet from his face. Blake froze, both mentally and physically. The snapping buzz rattled through the canyon and he thought he heard Big Luke's wicked laugh.

"Who's gonna get ya, Blake?!" he yelled, his coarse voice rolling through the dry air and carried on a deadly laugh. "Me or the snake?"

Blake watched the snake and it hadn't moved. Wyler had gained the height advantage on them now and he knew both he and Hank were covered. He would have to turn to get a shot at the snake and any movement would expose him to Wyler's fire or send the fangs sinking into the flesh of his face. Sweat poured from his forehead and into his eyes and they blurred with the salty sting.

Luke Wyler's massive body was rising, blue against blue in the clear desert sky. He was staring at Blake intently, raising the pistol and aiming it at the broad of his back. Blake heard the exploding shell and it sounded strangely distant and he waited for the awful, crushing impact. He caught a blur of blue out of the corner of his eye and waited for death. It seemed to him that it was taking forever for the bullet to travel such a short distance.

The snake watched him, eyes dry and unblinking. Blake heard a scream, gargling, blood-filled, and the clatter of a weapon on the rocks below, and he knew he wasn't dead. He rolled onto his back with the rifle on his chest and fired in the same instant. The snake hung momentarily, its head turned into a stump of flesh, then flopped backward to quiver and thrash as it slid down the wall.

Blake slumped against the rock, his heart thudding and blood pounding in his ears. He drew in several sharp, ragged breaths before wiping the sweat from his eyes and sitting up. Big Luke lay sprawled across the rocks, his body broken and still. Blake looked across the canyon and saw Rodrigo lower the rifle from his shoulder before turning the cavalry horse to face the detachment of soldiers encircling him on weary mounts.

Blake stared at the body of Luke Wyler and felt empty and weak as the hatred melted from his brain. It's over, he thought. Finally over. First Will, and now the Wyler brothers. They were brothers in killing and now they are brothers in death.

He struggled to his feet and slowly worked his way to where Hank stood, looking down at the captain lying baking in the burning sun.

## Chapter Eighteen

Colonel Bibby was still giving suicide some serious consideration as his horse, followed by Corporal Darby's, turned down the main street of Twin Buttes. Each step, every hoof placement, had been pure agony all the way from Fort Hastings, and he knew he had never suffered such a monstrous hangover in his entire life.

The sight of the stage, parked before the office and loading passengers, filled him with instant relief and he realized there was still something to live for. He even tried to smile, though such a small effort sent a renewed pounding through his temples, and nodded to those who would be his fellow travelers as though his head were precariously balanced on his sloping shoulders. He stepped down stiffly and moved into the office with wooden strides.

"Good morning, sir," he said to the man filling out paper lying on the counter top, "I'm Colonel Nevis Bibby, and I believe I have reservations for this stage?"

Luther Masters looked up and contempt filled his eyes. "Don't think so."

Bibby smiled now, forgetting the pain. "Certainly I have. Captain Stearns assured me that everything was in proper order."

"Sorry. This coach is full," Masters said, leaning down to his paperwork again.

"What?" Bibby shouted, the florid color returning to his previously ashen face. "There must be some mistake! There has to be a mistake! I distinctly remember Captain Stearns telling me . . ."

"And I distinctly remember being turned away at the gates of your precious fort."

"Turned away?"

Masters laid his pencil aside and touched his long fingers together, then to his chin and was entirely pleased to have the opportunity to explain.

"Yes, turned away. Your Captain Stearns said he would personally certify my voucher for your passage. I believed him and reserved a space for you. Then, I had the unfortunate experience of going out to your fort to collect and being turned away. Something about no civilians allowed inside the fort?" He smiled his satisfaction. "Well, on this particular run, there will be no military inside my stage."

"No, by God! No!" Bibby wailed, sinking against the counter for support. "This can't be happening. I have no chance of surviving another week with Captain Stearns."

"I'm sorry, Colonel. I made every effort to obtain passage for you. My daughter, Gloria, even tried to talk with the captain about it when he was in town, but your fine captain was incredibly rude, even arrogant. The next stage will be through one week from today. If you would like, I can arrange, cash only please, for your . . ."

But his words fell on deaf ears. Colonel Bibby was stumbling toward the door, his pudgy legs moving inanimately like stumps decaying in the forest.

Colonel Bibby didn't remember the ride back to the fort. He didn't want to remember it. He spent the entire time trying to figure out if he had enough courage to kill Captain Stearns. No, he concluded as the gates came into view, that's an entirely unsatisfactory solution. First of all, he knew he would have been squashed like an overly ripe tomato, and secondly, even if God had intervened in his behalf, that would only mean he would have to wait for another replacement. Without a doubt, Stearns, however bad he might be, was still the only hope. A drink's the answer, he decided, brightening with the thought. One drink and then he would confront the captain.

The sentry stopped them at the gate. "Captain Stearns is dead, sir," he said, with a mixture of relief and forced regret.

"What!"

"I'm sorry, sir. The captain, or whoever he was, is dead." He pointed toward Rodrigo. "He's the man who killed him."

"He can't be dead, man!" Bibby raged. "Who the hell's going to take over the fort if he's dead?! No, that is definitely out of the question. He doesn't have the rank to do that to me. Out of the way, soldier!"

The sentry stepped aside and Bibby clucked his horse into motion, steering the animal toward the group of men standing beside the wagon. He stared straight at Rodrigo and rage brought a high pink to his cheeks. *He's the one who got me into all this! Him and his goddamned rifles! I didn't poke my nose into his business, so why the hell does he have to . . .* his eyes fell upon the smashed body of the captain and he nearly fainted. The pink faded from his face and hangover gray rapidly filled the void. He stumbled as he stepped from his horse and leaned against the mount for support.

"Are you all right, Colonel?" Rodrigo asked, placing a hand lightly on Bibby's shoulder.

Bibby forced the two puffed slits in his face apart and shook his head sadly.

"No, sir, I am not all right. Definitely not all right. First I miss my stage and now Captain Stearns is dead. If you would be so kind as to explain some of this to me, I would be most grateful."

"Of course. But it's kind of complicated."

"How complicated?"

"Very."

"Then let's have a drink first," Bibby said, moving toward his quarters. "I don't know if you're on my side, their side or whoever's side, and quite frankly, I couldn't care less at this point. I think a drink or two might make hell's creation and whatever you have to say considerably more palatable."

"Lieutenant Ashford, Corporal Thatcher, Blake Evans and Hank Lane should be present when we talk, Colonel."

Colonel Bibby turned wearily in the doorway with an empty wave of his hand. "Bring them. And the mules and the donkeys and the chickens and the pigs. Bring the civilians and the Mexicans and all the privates in all the armies. I don't care. But right now, I want a drink. No, I *need* a drink."

Rodrigo collected all the people mentioned and they crowded into Bibby's quarters, and as they did so, they saw the colonel standing beside his bed with two empty whiskey bottles in his hands. He looked up and there was something nearing total anguish in his eyes.

"After all this, after everything that's happened today, and there isn't a drink in the whole damned place." He shook his head sadly and stared at the bottles as though they were dead friends. "I don't know what I did to deserve this, but the big general in the sky is really giving me hell."

Rodrigo chuckled. "Maybe you'll have to face this one sober, Colonel. Worse things could happen."

"I don't know what," Bibby sighed as he sank onto his cot. "Okay. If I have to know, we might as well begin."

"Captain Stearns wasn't Captain Stearns. He was Colonel Jason T. Burke, Army of the Confederacy."

Bibby looked up and blinked his watery eyes. "I'm sorry, sir. I heard what you said, and I'm willing to hear more, but this just isn't working out. Corporal Darby!"

"Yes, sir?" Darby said, stepping in from his position outside the door.

"Son, you're looking at an old man who needs your help. Go to the barracks, the quartermaster stores, the stables, anywhere that the troops might have been drinking last night. Bring whatever you can find and make it double time. We will wait here for you."

"Whiskey or beer, sir?"

"Either, both or all, damnit! Move!"

"Yes, sir!"

Rodrigo rolled a cigarette and passed the makings around while they waited. Colonel Bibby stared out the window as if he were alone, lifeless, wilted, consumed by fate.

The corporal's boots pounded on the steps as he returned and Bibby's head moved in a slow orbit. He saw the full quart of whiskey in Darby's hand and life returned to his eyes. He nodded toward some glasses. "Pour, son. One for everybody, and one for yourself, if you like."

"Yes, sir!" Darby said, filling the glasses and handing them around before pouring one for himself. "But I'm on duty, sir?" he asked cautiously.

The glass moved to Bibby's lips in quivering fingertips. "Take the day off, son. We're all taking the day off. Maybe tomorrow too." He drank, closed his eyes and savored the taste before opening them again and looking at Rodrigo. "I'll thank you, sir, for repeating what you said earlier. I shall be the paragon of interest now."

Rodrigo explained about the first ambush, how the real Captain Stearns had been killed, who the Wyler brothers were, what the plan had been, about the second ambush of the Frenchman, how he had lured Burke into the desert, how his men had drawn Lieutenant Ashford from the scene, and how Corporal Thatcher had co-operated.

Colonel Bibby listened, sipping his drink and gazing out the window throughout. When Rodrigo had finished, he studied what he had heard in momentary silence before turning to the Argentinian.

"Out of all that, and all we have to show for it is one miserable Confederate private?"

"You don't even have that, Colonel. Four thousand of Maximilian's money goes to him, as well as your putting through for an honorable discharge for him in Corporal Thatcher's name. I promised him that for his co-operation, without which, Burke would be commandant of this fort and, eventually, your military career would be ruined."

Bibby's eyebrows raised heavily. "Career? This isn't a career, it's a life sentence."

"It might not be that bleak, Colonel," Rodrigo said with a light chuckle. "Lieutenant Ashford conducted himself well today. As well as any captain might have. As a full colonel, I'd think you would have the authority to make a battlefield promotion."

Bibby's face brightened as though a strong flame were being drawn slowly nearer his head, and he listened more intently as Rodrigo continued.

"He would probably even make a fine commandant for Fort Hastings, if you sent the proper telegrams."

Bibby was rising from the bed now like a great balloon being filled with hot air. He placed his drink on the nightstand, but his eyes were on Ashford. His knuckles crept up the small of his back to rest against his spine. He crossed the room once to test his step, then turned again to Ashford.

"Mr. Ashford, there are many things that have to be done, and I suggest you finish your drink and get cracking. The dead have to be buried, an escort arranged for these men and their weapons to Mexico, the barracks has to be cleaned and troops inspected, etcetera and so forth." He paused and smiled. "If you would be so kind as to attend to those details . . . Captain?"

Ashford gulped his drink in a single swallow. "Yes, sir!" he said, snapping a salute as he backed toward the door. "On the double, sir!"

Bibby responded with a desultory wave of his hand.

"Corporal Darby!"

"Yes, sir?"

"Get fresh mounts for you and me."

"Yes, sir. Where are we going, sir?"

"To town, man, to town! I've got some telegrams to send. But, before you get the horses, draw enough money from the paymaster to cover stage expenses from here to San Francisco." He paused and his eyes shone. "One-way fare is all I'm interested in." He turned to Rodrigo. "Now, how long is it going to take to clear up this unfortunate business about the rifles?"

"I give you ten thousand dollars, my agreed-upon price with General Strickland, and you give me the rifles and a receipt."

"Consider it done," Bibby said, striding toward his desk with renewed vigor.

They stopped just outside the gates and watched the wagon, led by six Mexicans and escorted to the rear by twenty-five cavalry troops, follow its lumbering course to the south.

The four of them were silent for nearly a minute before Rodrigo looked first at Blake, then Hank. "Are you sure you won't come with us? Hank?"

"Naw, Rod. Thanks just the same. I've got some unfinished business to tend to in New Orleans."

Rodrigo nodded with a knowing smile. "Blake?"

"Do you need our help?"

"No. We can manage now that we have the weapons."

"Then I guess I'd better trail along with Hank. Seems like he gets himself into a little more trouble than one man can handle."

"I understand."

Rodrigo leaned forward and extended his hand, as did Munn, using his left with the white bandage a stark contrast around his tanned chest. They shook four ways then Rodrigo reached into his vest pocket and handed a wad of bills to Hank.

"What's this for?" Hank asked, holding the money extended.

"After Tully got his, and I paid for the rifles, there was a thousand left over. You and Blake can split it."

Blake and Hank started to protest, but Rodrigo and Munn turned their horses and pressed them into a slow gallop. Rodrigo twisted in the saddle and called over his shoulder, "The four of us are partners in The Lucky Lady now. Dig deep!"

Biggie Munn waved and they were gone.

Hank stared at the money before peeling off half. "We'll drink on Maximilian tonight."

"How much money are we going to need in New Orleans?" Blake asked, stuffing the money in his shirt pocket.

"Much as we can get. Why?"

"Then we might as well pick up another seventy-five hundred."

"What?"

"Seventy-five hundred."

"How?"

"Telegram."

"To who, damnit?"

"To the warden at Little Rock Federal Penitentiary. There was a twenty-five-hundred-dollar reward on each member of the Wyler gang. All we need is a telegram from Colonel Bibby and it's ours."

Colonel Bibby and Corporal Darby were just cantering from the fort and turning toward town.

"Oh, Colonel Bibby?" Hank called.

The horses stopped and turned.

"Yes?"

"Mind if we ride into town with you? There's another telegram for you to send."

Bibby shrugged as he urged his mount toward town again. "Come along, but let's make haste. Who knows what miserable things can happen in the next week."

Blake moved up beside Hank and they followed at a leisurely pace. "Hank," he asked, looking across, "I've been wondering about something. Do you think that rock we found in the bottom of The Lucky Lady was really silver?"

"Naw. Just another dumb, ugly, heavy rock, like I told you before."

"Think we should take another look on our way out?"

"Hell no. Besides, with eighty-five hundred dollars, what do we need with an empty hole in the desert?"

"Just a thought. A little clean shovelin' wouldn't hurt us none, just to make sure."

"There is no such thing as clean shovelin', Blake, and none that don't hurt. Forget it. I've got big plans for us in New Orleans."

Blake sighed and leaned back in the saddle.

"I'll bet you do, Hank. I'll just bet you do."

FIC Bjo         Bjorgum, K
The desert sentinels /
BKM  AF   1st ed.           1980.

Athens Regional Library System

3 3207 00103 0743

ECS
ES
Books

## DATE DUE

| | | | |
|---|---|---|---|
| NOV 24 '80 | OC 4 '83 | NOV 4 1991 | |
| FE 3 '81 | NO 1 '83 | JAN 8 REC'D | |
| AP 8 '81 | NO 30 83 | | |
| JE 4 '81 | MR 1 '84 | | |
| OCT 28 1981 | FE 25 '84 | | |
| DEC 8 1981 | MR 8 '84 | | |
| MAR 8 1982 | OCT 29 1984 | | |
| APR 13 1982 | DEC 10 1984 | | |
| JUN 8 1982 | FEB 4 1985 | | |
| OCT 5 1982 | AP 18 '85 | | |
| DE 1 '82 | NOV 25 1985 | | |
| FE 9 '83 | AUG 1986 | | |
| JAN 26 | OC 07 '86 | | |
| FEB 17 | NO 18 '86 | | |
| AP 25 '83 | JUL 12 1988 | | |
| MY 2 '83 | AP 24 '89 | | |
| JE 3 '83 | NOV 13 1989 | | |
| AG 17 '83 | AUG 6 1990 | | |

GAYLORD                                    PRINTED IN U.S.A.